CW01640556

Bartender

BEEFCAKE

L. MOONE

Cover art by eXplicitTales

Published by eXplicitTales

ISBN-13: 9781913930936

CONTENTS

CHAPTER ONE

*** Jane ***

Sometimes when I glance over at him, I find that he's already looking. Or is he? Maybe it was just a coincidence and I'm reading too much into it as usual. But what if…

Nahhh. Big Bartender-BB-as I've come to refer to him in my thoughts, is so effortlessly cool; my polar opposite. So well put together. With his perfectly styled beard, fashionably messy haircut, tattoos, and pierced eyebrow. Even the clothes he wears are just a little bit different. It's mostly just jeans and t-shirts, and the obligatory button down shirt with rolled up sleeves. Swoon.

No matter what the late October weather brings, he's never wearing anything more than that and he always has his deliciously thick forearms out. Still, everything always just looks right. Like he's put some thought behind it, and picked out just the right watch or chunky bracelet to go with each outfit. Or maybe it's because they drape over his substantial frame so seductively, I can't stop myself from picturing what's underneath, or wondering how warm his skin would feel beneath my touch.

And it's not just his look that speaks to me… He's so worldly and sharp. Can hold a conversation on any topic and sound authoritative and confident. BB is a smooth talker, but not a bullshitter. I could listen to him from afar all night.

Meanwhile, I'm just… me. A bit boring, a lot bookish, but only when it comes to genre fiction. They might call me the Romance Queen back at Teddington Public Library where I work, with a near perfect track record of being able to recall book titles based on just a few key plot details, but none of that matters in the real world. None of that would ever impress him; he probably thinks romance novels are childish… But they're my way to escape reality and experience the passion I crave every time I lay eyes on him.

My reading preferences haven't translated into real life love anyway… Not even once.

No, if we ever spoke, he'd lose interest quite quickly. Like how I've seen him shut down other people once he realized they weren't worth his time.

He's educated and well read. Knows about business and the economy and tech. And I can't even figure out half of the features on the phone I've had for two years. Even if he looks at me every so often, he'd stop as soon as he knew how inept I am at basically everything other than my job. More so once he finds out how hopelessly infatuated I am with him. Desperation is a bad look 100% of the time.

I've spent too many long nights in this pub. Ever since I ended up here with Vicky from work and a few of her friends, I haven't been able to stay away. I don't even order any alcohol, just a Virgin Mojito or something similar, even when I'd much rather have a hot chocolate. Unfortunately pubs don't serve those.

And I try to time my orders in such a way that he's busy with other customers, like right now. That way I don't have to face the inevitable disappointment of losing this dream. This fantasy.

Of everything that could have been, if only I wasn't myself, and he wasn't so ridiculously out of my league…

*** Nathan ***

She's a dream. Beautiful, but doesn't seem to realize it. With shapely legs in skinny jeans leading up to the perfectly full hourglass figure hidden beneath that loose knit sweater. Effortlessly elegant, no matter how simple her outfit is on any given day.

Behind those adorable red-rimmed glasses, she has the sparkliest amber eyes. Nothing escapes her notice. Whenever I try to steal a glance in her direction, she's already looking.

She can tell how obsessed I am. That's why she

prefers to order her drinks from Alexis, or whoever else is working alongside me on any given night. She knows that no matter how hard I try to put up a stoic front, there's chaos inside. So many conflicting voices, telling me all sorts of sordid things.

I want to bend her over the counter and have my way with her, and at the same time, cradle her in my arms and whisper sweet nothings in her ear. I'd tell her that as long as I'm around, I'll do anything I can to make her happy. To keep her safe. To let nothing bad happen to her, ever. Except, I am the bad one. Who will protect her from me?

If by some kind of magic, the pub would empty right now, and I got her all to myself, there's no telling what I'd want to do. How could I resist her siren call?

As much as I've read and learned over the years, about philosophy and meditation and all that other stuff, I can't implement any of it around her. I can't shut down these dirty thoughts. I can't control the fact that I get a semi every time I see her come in… I can't help but stare at her, imagining all the beauty that's hidden beneath the many layers of warm clothes she likes to wrap herself up in. It's a constant fight against the desperate urge to strike up a conversation. It's hopeless. She's repulsed by me, as she should be. I am what's wrong with this world. I'm unworthy of her attention. She's a ten, whereas I'm a three at most. Maybe a five if I lost fifty pounds. Not that I haven't tried that... Hell, even if I had the perfect gym bod, I'd still be punching above my worth with her.

I try to focus on the cocktail order I've already been given, knowing full well that she's going to take the opportunity to order something right now while I'm busy. That's what she always does. Avoids me. Perhaps it's for the best. Because if we came face to face right now, I don't know if I could be coherent. What would I even say?

"Hey Nathan, you're on your own for an hour," Alexis tells me. "Gotta go tuck the little one in."

"All right, take your time," I reply.

I watch her hang up her apron and slip out towards the stairs leading to the upstairs apartment. Alexis runs this place together with her husband, Bob, so she's the boss. While he's more of a behind the scenes kind of guy, she's right here behind the bar every single night. It must be challenging, continuing to work this hard with a baby, but Alexis is tough as nails and I have to admire that about her.

Only then do I steal a glance in *her* direction. My mystery woman. Our eyes meet. This is it. She hasn't ordered her one drink for the evening yet, and I'm the only one manning the bar...

I rush to finish preparing the round of margaritas for the group of cheerful fifty-something ladies that ordered first. Then, I take a deep breath and turn towards my mark. All or nothing, here we go.

"Hi, can I get you anything?"

She stares at me for a second, then glances left and right, as if she's desperate to get away. I'm no prize by any means, but her obvious rejection hurts anyway. I've just asked for her order, not for her to marry me, for fuck's sake.

"I, umm…" She trains her eyes on me again, and there's a hint of softness in her gaze that soothes my broken ego. "I haven't really decided yet."

"Okay…" I'm about to turn away when her hand reaches over the counter and lands right beside mine. So close, I feel her warmth right beside my little finger. My heart just about stops.

"What's your signature cocktail?" she asks.

Ah, so *this* is the game we're playing. Hell yes!

"Not in the mood for a Virgin Mojito tonight?" I ask.

She briefly presses her lips together. "You remember my regular order?"

Even though I never served her? Yeah. I do. I remember every last detail about her.

I shrug off her question. "Photographic memory."

For a brief moment, she averts her gaze to her hand, still resting next to mine, our pinkies touching ever so briefly. She twitches, but doesn't pull it away. "It's Friday Night. I don't think a Virgin- *anything* is going to cut it."

I nod, and try not to smile. "Okay, I think I can figure something out."

"Thanks," she says. Those rose pink lips. It's hard not to stare when she speaks. Wonder what else is rose pink on her… *Holy hell, shut the fuck up!*

It's time to rise to the challenge, just not *like that.* Just when I figure things can't get any more uncomfortable, the margarita group makes a move on an empty table further away from the bar, and it's just her and me left at this end of the counter.

I know how much she likes Virgin Mojitos, because that's what she usually orders. Serving her a normal Mojito would be way too obvious, so I quickly wrack my brain for cocktails with a similarly refreshing flavor profile; preferably something off-menu, to show that I can do a lot more than tap beer or open bottles of cider straight from the fridge… If this is the challenge she has given me, I'm intent on passing it with flying colors. This might be the only chance I'll ever get to impress this woman.

Her eyes are on me, I feel them. I have to try very hard not to let it throw me off my game.

Within minutes, I combine white rum, lime juice, Chartreuse, syrup, and ice in a cocktail shaker and give it a good, vigorous shake. The end result is a beautifully lime-colored elixir, ready to be strained into a dainty coupe glass and topped with soda and a garnish of fresh mint. It looks a lot more high class than the rest of this historic West London pub.

When I slide the glass over to her, I feel the tickle of a bead of sweat near my temple. I could make hundreds of these a night and never break a sweat, but this time… It's all the nerves of having her watch me while I do my thing.

I watch as she picks up the glass for her first taste. Time seems to freeze, more so since we're still the only ones at the bar. Surprising, for what ought to be the busiest night of the week. I hope she loves it. Oh god, please make her love it!

"Oh, wow," she says with a smile. "This is delicious! What's it called?"

"Daisy de Santiago. It's a classic Cuban cocktail as well, like the Mojito."

"I must remember the name, so I can order it again next time," she muses.

I lean forward just a little. "Don't worry about it; I'll remember it for you."

"Photographic memory, huh?" she asks.

When it comes to you, yes.

Her cheeks turn a few shades darker and she averts her gaze. Shit, did I just say that out loud? Still, she doesn't turn away. Blushing is usually a good sign, isn't it?

"I hope you made enough for two?" she asks, an awkward couple of seconds later.

"It's better when it's fresh. If you want another, just say the word."

She subtly shakes her head. "I meant for you to join me. It's a rather quiet evening, anyway."

Could it be? Is she actually flirting back?

CHAPTER TWO

*** Jane ***

Holy shit. Did I really just say that?

It's not liquid courage, since I've only had one sip. But I feel brave, anyway. Ever since BB asked me for my order, there's something about him pulling me in. A certain magnetism, attracting me like a moth to a flame.

It's an apt comparison. I'm the boring moth, whereas he's fire. Hot, beautiful, irresistible, and also dangerous. Because I could get hurt. I will get my heart broken, sooner rather than later. Because this little dance we're doing is just friendly banter to him. Just something you do as a bartender with your customers. For me, it's something else entirely because I don't banter. I just read about it in romantic comedies.

How would that comparison go? I'm the slightly nerdy Plain Jane heroine, and he's… He's everything. The bad boy with a heart of gold. The confident alpha who sweeps me off my feet with a mere look. With the broad shoulders and the thick forearms sticking out from his rolled up shirt sleeve... Dad bod romances are a thing now, for which I am grateful. And this guy is the whole package. Hopefully, with a big package to complete the fantasy.

Oh shut up! You're not that kind of girl!

I would like to be, though. Just this once. The kind of girl to seduce the hot bartender for a night of passion under the stars. If only I could break through my inner critic and take a chance on something otherworldly and wild.

I take another sip. Delicious as it is, it's also rather strong. I'm not much of a drinker, and I'm getting a slight buzz already. Or maybe that's just because he's still looking at me. His large hand resting on the bar counter in front of me, begging to be grabbed. Swirls of black ink peep out from underneath the sleeve of his shirt as if to invite me to stare some more.

"Love your tattoo," I mumble. Shit, did I just say *that*?

"Do you have any?" he asks, his eyes trained on me so intently, I daren't look away too far.

"Maybe I'll let you find out," I whisper, biting my bottom lip.

God, our entire exchange is straight out of one of the steamier books I've read lately. Awkward, and yet... At least they offered me a roadmap for what to say. Because it seems to be working so far. Maybe I will find out what it's like to be *that kind of girl,* just this once.

I'll get this attraction out of my system just in time for when he inevitably realizes how boring I actually am and loses interest in me. All for the experience of a lifetime, or so I hope.

When I look up into his eyes, I find that his stare intensifies. It's unnerving, but also… kind of empowering. I have him hooked. Shit, I never knew I could do that, with what? A couple of suggestive remarks thrown his way? This is way too easy.

"You're lucky Alexis just left me alone behind the bar, or I'd take you up on that offer right now in the store room," he fires back.

A shiver runs all the way down the back of my neck and spine. Now I know. When people do dumb shit and then say: 'One thing led to another'...*This* . *This* is what they mean. I could happily let one thing turn into another with this man right here. No matter how wrong and dirty it is.

Is this what life is like for these other people? Like Big Bartender over here. Is this what his Friday nights are like for him, normally? How many exchanges like this has he got himself into in the past? How many times has flirtatious banter turned into something real for him? He's a natural. He has no clue how fucking nervous I am, or how much I fake it.

"You mean unlucky," I breathe.

Oh man, I wish I'd at least worn matching

underwear this morning. At least something pretty, rather than a boring gray t-shirt bra and my trusty No-VPL boy shorts.

God, I really am hopeless. I never thought this could happen. Or rather, that I could make it happen just with a few strategic sentences. Maybe seduction really is a skill that can be learned, rather than an innate talent… Who could have known? Why have I never tried this before? Maybe got some practice in with a guy I didn't feel so strongly about. Why am I always behind the curve?

*** Nathan ***

Wow, that escalated quickly. Within minutes, we went from me mixing her a drink to quick-fire flirtations and teases.

"You mean unlucky," she whispers, and I just about come in my pants.

This isn't supposed to happen to me. And certainly not with her. I thought she was about ready to run when I asked her for her order, and now… Now I'm the one in a good mood to bolt.

Because it can only go downhill from here. Sooner or later she'll come to her senses and realize that this is a dumbass idea, and I'm unworthy of her time or attention. Things are all fine and well now, but at some point my mask will inevitably slip. That's when she'll change her mind.

I put a certain amount of effort into looking nice when I'm dressed, but I haven't been able to do much about what's underneath. I'm no match for her. Just a chubby average Joe who tries to make up for his shortcomings with statement shirts, nice watches, and semi-intellectual books on my shelves at home. Just a guy who has eyed this woman for a whole month, without ever having the balls to say hello, until just now.

She's everything.

And she still stares at me from underneath those thick dark lashes, waiting for me to come back with something clever to ratchet up the tension some more. I've got nothing. Nothing, except the truth.

"I get off at midnight," I tell her. The innuendo in that statement is lost on me until I see the corner of her mouth flutter.

"Hopefully, so will I."

Good lord, make this sweet torture end!

And just like that, a large group of new patrons approaches the bar and orders one complicated drink after another. And I can't do much else except try to focus on my work and steal glances at *her* as often as I can.

Every time I do, I find her already looking. And my whole body remains on edge, buzzing with so much tension, I'm about ready to explode. It's going to be a long three hours until the end of my shift…

*** Jane ***

Time creeps slowly, and passes too quickly all at once. Because now that I have his attention and his permission in a way, I could spend an eternity staring at him while he does his thing.

Even just observing him tap a pint is an event, because it's him. The hot bartender of my dreams.

I nurse my drink for as long as I can, and in between other orders, BB refills it without me having to ask. Because he's looking at me too, as much as possible. I don't need to speculate about it anymore; it's blatantly obvious. He's looking, and hopefully fantasizing. His colleague comes back for an hour or so, and even when she tries to make conversation with him in between orders, he barely looks in her direction, because he's so distracted.

I see it in the slight flush on his face. The erratic movements his hand makes every so often when our eyes meet. He's excited, or maybe nervous? Is he as turned on as I am?

Every little thing I feel, I project onto him and he reflects it back to me. Hours pass, but the tension never does. It stays, and keeps building.

By the time the bar empties, my heart races uncontrollably. I probably should have gone to the restroom a while back, because it's urgent. It's five to twelve, and I seize the opportunity before I miss my window.

By the time I'm done freshening up, applying a fresh coat of lipstick and fixing my hair, it's one minute past twelve. I return to find my favorite bartender alone and wiping down the counter. He raises his head when I take my seat opposite him again.

"I thought you changed your mind," he says.

I shake my head once. "Never."

Still, there's something different in him. Like the spell is broken, and suddenly, our genius idea of 'getting off at twelve' doesn't seem so grand anymore. I slip off the bar stool, and pause there, just three feet away from him. I'm in a good mood to bolt now, if only my knees weren't shaking.

"Look," he says, training his eyes on mine for just a second.

I press my lips together tightly, just to stop myself from falling apart with nerves.

"I can't do this."

"It's okay," I whisper.

He shakes his head. "No. No, it's not."

"No, it's not," I repeat. I guess seduction was a talent after all, and not a skill you learn from a few books. Whatever it is, I don't possess it. I flew too close to the sun, and got burned sooner than expected.

"I can't take you into the store room and do whatever we hinted at earlier," he says.

My throat closes up, though I'm trying to play it cool. "You have a girlfriend, I understand."

He shakes his head. "No, I don't."

"You don't?" I try to breathe. You just don't want *me.* Of course he doesn't. I mean, look at him. He's cool and suave and I'm… Me.

"I don't want you like that… you know?" He looks at me apologetically. His dark brown eyes are so kind and warm, so honest. It's the absolute worst.

I shrug and adjust my glasses. "It's okay." It was a nice fantasy while it lasted. And now it's time to wake up and smell the disappointment. My earlier comparison still stands. I'm the moth, and he's the flame. And now, I die. Figuratively.

"If we spend the night together now…" he starts.

The blood rushing in my ears makes it hard to listen to what he has to say. God, I want to run. Anything just to make this feeling stop.

"I won't have it in me to say goodbye in the morning," he says at last.

I frown and shake my head. "I don't get it."

He sighs deeply and runs his hand through his hair. His irresistibly full hair. I wish to know what that feels like against my fingertips. Or indeed, between my thighs… *Shut up with those dirty, dirty thoughts, woman!*

"I can't just- I can't be casual about this, you understand?" he asks.

I shake my head again. "Not really, no."

"I…" He leans forward and rests his much larger hand right next to mine. Exactly the move I made when I ordered my drink a few hours ago. It's unnerving as well as comforting and extremely fucking confusing. My pinky twitches involuntarily, and brushes past his, taking my breath away so completely, I feel faint.

"I don't just want a one night stand with you." His voice is so flat, it's almost inaudible.

This whole situation is backward. Men are supposed to jump head-first at the chance of whatever is about to happen here. *I'm* supposed to be the one to have reservations about falling into bed with a complete stranger, not the other way around!

"Then what *do* you want?" I blurt out. Clearly, I'm a glutton for punishment and need my rejections spelled out to me in detail.

"I want a chance to get to know you. *Completely*."

I blink a few times. I've read this line somewhere, quite recently. But the context doesn't match. In the book, the hero got down on one knee and proposed after this. Clearly, that's not what's happening here. He's just trying to- I don't know what the hell he's trying anymore.

"There's nothing much to know," I say.

"I very much doubt that's true." He gazes at me again, and the conflicted look in his eyes just about melts my panties off. How am I still this hopelessly attracted to him when he does his best to douse the fire?

The silence growing between us while I stare at his pleading eyes in shock and confusion is utterly painful.

He swallows hard. "Give me a chance?"

Without thinking, I blurt out the first thing that pops into my mind. "I'd give you *anything*."

Jesus, can I just get through a conversation without making a complete fool of myself by spouting clichés? That's what I get for drinking those deceptively pretty cocktails.

He smiles briefly, then glances down at my lips, just as the bottom one starts to quiver. This is so excruciatingly weird; I don't know how to break the tension anymore. All the romance novels in the world couldn't prepare me for this moment. He has well and truly called my bluff and I don't know what happens next anymore. Because this isn't me. It has never been me. Good girls don't do this; they don't flirt with hot men in bars late at night. I should have known better than to try. Now I deserve all the heartache that's coming to me. That's what I get for leading him on.

CHAPTER THREE

*** Nathan ***

Holy hell, just how am I supposed to be sensible and resist her when she keeps saying things like this? We haven't even done anything yet, and this girl screws up my feelings so badly, I wouldn't know how to ever let her go. I'm rushing headfirst into my own doom, and all she seems to want to do is egg me on.

"How about we start with your name and phone number?" I ask.

My banal question is instantly punished by the dumbfounded expression on her face. "So you can let me down with excuses by text?"

It's my turn to be confused. "Wait, what do you think is happening here?" I ask.

She sighs and shakes her head. "We got carried away earlier, and now you're looking for a way out."

Something comes over me; bravery or stupidity, I can't quite tell. I take her hand and try not to get overwhelmed by all the sensations our touch inspires. "Sweetheart, I'm looking for a way *in*. Not out."

"You got in three hours ago; all you have to do is

follow through."

She's too much. All my good sense has run out. I lean across the counter as best I can, placing my hand on her cheek. The rest happens almost on autopilot.

Her eyes flicker up at me, eyebrows pulled together in anticipation. I lick my bottom lip as I bring her face closer to me, both of us now leaning across the bar counter to meet roughly halfway. Her lips are barely an inch away from mine, truncated breaths caress my beard.

I can't wait. I can't think. I must know if she tastes as sweet as she smells. Like jasmine and honey, an apt comparison to match the warm shimmer in her eyes.

She meets me the rest of the way, pressing her mouth to mine for a moment before retreating. I wrap my hand around the back of her neck, my fingers burying themselves in the soft locks of her dark blonde hair.

From my lips to hers, I try to tell her everything I failed to express earlier. Just how many times I played out this very moment in my head.

She's sweet perfection, how she seems to melt against the counter. That wretched thing is horribly in the way. I've sported a semi all night, but as soon as I got my first taste of her, I'm raging for more.

I know I said I couldn't just take her into the back room and have my way with her, but… My cock didn't get the message. It's on now. My defenses have fallen.

Pulling away for a deep breath, I take a moment to admire her. Eyes half shut and lips parted with a desperate sigh, she's a vision of beauty. In a few long strides, I meet her on her side of the bar and cup her face again. Our height difference is more evident now. Even though she's sitting on a tall stool, I've still got a couple of inches on her.

"Still want me to follow through, darling?" My voice is raspy when I ask the question.

She doesn't speak, but her denim clad legs part to allow me closer access. I can't resist the invitation and kiss her again, this time introducing a little tongue, stifling a gasp in the back of her throat.

Her arms end up around my neck, fingers brush through my hair. It feels so good, sending tremors through my spine and encouraging me to get even closer.

Our bodies merge, the curve of her full breasts pressing up against my chest, sending my heart rate into overdrive. All my best intentions have flown out the window. Now that this train is in motion, nothing can stop it anymore.

*** Jane ***

This is it. Everything I've wanted. The culmination of a whole month of silent yearning.

His lips are fire and his hands determined. He sets

me alight from the inside out, and fans the flames with the tip of his tongue.

I'm so overwhelmed, I'm floating, like this moment couldn't possibly get any better. There isn't any time to wonder if I'm doing this right. Does technique even matter, or is it just instinct?

His strong hands roam my back, kneading the tension out of my shoulders until I'm reduced to a puddle of jelly.

I scoot forward in my seat, eager to see what other wonders I've missed out on in my twenty-seven years on this planet. He feels solid and powerful, like nothing can move him or faze him. With him by my side, I'd be safe and nothing could hurt me. Except… He could. He could snap me like a twig. That makes this even hotter. And more terrifying.

I get close enough for the hard bulge in his jeans to brush against my crotch, sending shockwaves down into my core. There's no mistaking what this is, what it means. It's happening. He's ready. Everything we teased at is about to come true.

I was already damp down there, but now I'm gushing. It's all for him. It's only ever been for him. No man has ever touched me there, or anywhere else for that matter. Except one… but that didn't count and I don't care to remember it.

And… God, I need him to be serious about me. Despite all my words to the contrary, I don't want *this.* A quick and dirty screw in an empty pub after hours.

Men are animals; just after one thing, a voice of the past rings in my ears. *You can't give in to temptation. Or you're just as bad as they are.*

Why? Why these thoughts? Why after all these years? This is the 21st century, for Pete's sake. Men and women are equals in every possible way. If men can seek out pleasure, why can't I? My body is ready. I feel it on every inch of my skin. I want it. I want him. I want what's in those jeans. I want him to fill me up. But I also… Don't.

The disappointment is immense.

"Hey…" His concerned voice snaps me out of my trance. "What's wrong?"

I shake my head, because I can't bring myself to tell him. I also can't shake how dirty I feel. God, I've been so stupid. I actually thought I could do this. I got him this riled up, and now I'm pulling the plug? That's ridiculous, as well as hugely unfair to both of us. Bloody great timing for me to freak out and ruin it all.

I take a deep breath, trying to shake off all these conflicting thoughts, but…

My heart has already sunk. All the steamy romance in the world couldn't prepare me for this. I'm not that girl. And I'm certainly not getting my night of passion under the stars. Beginnings of tears prickle in my eye, just as my arms lose the strength to hold onto him.

"I'm sorry." I have to force out the words, because this time, my throat actually closes up all the way.

The confusion in his eyes is too painful to look at. He must be wondering what he's done wrong. How do I make it clear that he hasn't? He's perfect, more than I could've asked for. But I'm deathly afraid of what this means, for me as well as us. I'm too terrified to explain the truth. If he knew who I really am, that I've never willingly let anyone get this close to me before, he'd laugh at me. Or worse, pity me. I couldn't stomach that. I'd be better off remembering what he told me earlier. He was interested; he wanted a way in. He *liked me back*. Damnit.

"Hey, darling... We don't have to move so quickly." His deep voice is like a soothing balm on my soul, and fuel to the fire in my crotch all at once. When he takes a step away from me, my body seems to scream at the loss of his affections. So close. I came so close to getting everything I crave. So close to filling the gaping hole in my heart. I almost had him; the star of every naughty dream I've had since I first saw him. I finally got over myself and seduced him. And it worked, too!

And then, I just had to go and mess it all up.

"I thought..." I try to formulate a complete thought, but nothing sensible comes. "It's not you, it's me."

Argh, that's also such a dumb thing to say. Whenever I read that in a book, I tend to roll my eyes, because it usually means the opposite. In this case, it's actually true.

He reaches for my chin, and tilts my head up. His eyes, still dark with desire, burn down into mine. I can't bear to look at them for more than a brief moment.

Despite his very obvious arousal, he forces a smile and backs up. "Shhh… It's okay."

I shake my head. No. No, it's not. Nothing is ever going to be okay.

"I…" My eyes dart around the otherwise empty bar. Shit, I'm here all alone. I'm such an idiot for putting myself in this position. Nobody even knows I'm here. Literally anything could have happened, and it would have all been my fault. "I have to go."

He raises his hands up in defense. I quickly grab my bag and coat and make a run for it, straight for the double entrance doors. I push my way through, and blinded by the mist on my glasses, I crash headfirst into a concrete wall, or something like it.

"Careful there, missy." Two giant hands keep me steady, preventing my otherwise inevitable fall to the ground. Shit. The bouncer. Argh! As if this moment couldn't get any more humiliating.

"Crap, I'm so sorry," I stammer.

"No harm done." He lets go of me and I blink a

few times, trying to find my bearings. Right. Home's that way. My legs carry me away in long, be it slightly shaky strides. But with every step, a little piece of myself gets left behind.

*** Nathan ***

"-the hell did you do?" Dean's voice booms at me, making me flinch at its intensity. Fucking great. This is what I was missing; a judgy audience to witness my fall from grace.

"Nothing. I didn't do anything!" I say. I didn't, right? Nothing she didn't enthusiastically consent to first?

"That didn't look like fucking nothing!" he argues. "The girl was crying, for fuck's sake!"

The door squeaks behind him, and for a split second, I'm convinced she's back. My mystery woman with the red rimmed glasses. Giving me a second chance I don't deserve.

It's not her, though. It's Dean's girlfriend, Megan, sporting a puzzled expression on her face.

"What's going on here?" She props her hands up on her hips and looks us over with fiery black eyes. "Are you guys having a literal fight right now? Oh my God!"

"No way," I say. I might be humiliated, but I'm not suicidal. "Nothing happened!"

Dean just grunts, but doesn't stop glaring at me.

"Okay, well, if you're done with whatever this is, maybe we can grab a bite to eat. I'm starving. Dean?" Megan tugs at Dean's arm, who remains immovable, but just for a second or so.

I'm far from a coward, but Dean isn't your usual rowdy patron requiring to be put in his place. He's built like a wardrobe, with the demeanor to match. And I'd really rather not get into it with him.

"Fine. But this isn't over," Dean threatens in a half-whisper. "Tomorrow we're going to have a little chat about this, you and I. After everything that happened here six months ago, I figured you'd know better."

Now he equates me to the creep who roofied Megan's friend here in April. Seriously, fuck my life.

I watch as he turns around and greets his girl with a kiss to the forehead. Within a split second, he sheds his scary bouncer mask and is tenderness personified. Seeing their little exchange, and the gooey sweet looks they give each other, makes me feel even worse.

That's what I wanted with her, my mystery woman. Someone to come home to. To cuddle in front of the TV with after a late shift. To hug and kiss and cherish forever… Instead, she ran. She fucking fled!

Does my breath stink? Am I that repulsive up close? What the fuck did I do wrong?

Everything was going brilliantly. She was ready and

willing. She essentially eye fucked me for hours. And the moment I put my hands on her, she froze up like she saw a spider crawl up her arm.

It's not you, it's me, she said. Really? Has anyone ever said that phrase and meant it literally? I don't even know the first thing about her, and yet she has torn me up inside. This isn't right. I can't let this stand. Maybe if I can just talk to her again and figure out what really happened, I can make sense of it all…

I rush to grab my coat. "Gotta go, sorry. Tell Alexis I'll do the stock taking ahead of tomorrow's shift," I tell Dean.

Before he has the chance to respond or stop me, I'm already out the door. Now… Which way did she go? The dark streets, including the bus stop down the road are empty, except for a couple walking arm in arm about twenty feet away. Maybe they saw where she went?

This may be my only chance to figure this out. I'm going to have to make it count.

CHAPTER FOUR

*** Jane ***

Is it still a hangover if you haven't slept at all? I don't know. After tossing and turning all night, with hot glimpses of our brief kiss flashing before my eyes and setting my nether regions on fire again, I don't know anything this morning. Except that I'm deeply ashamed of myself.

My eyes burn as I stare at the trolley with the pile of returned books, wondering if this pounding headache is ever going to stop. Thankfully the library closes a little early on Saturdays, or I'd never survive today's shift.

That's it. I'm never drinking again. Which is just as well, because I can never go back to the White Hart anyway. To face BB now would be… It would actually murder what little remains of my dignity. Jesus, what must he think of me right now? I led him on for hours, only to-

"Jane, sweetie, are you okay?" a concerned voice chirps behind me.

I huff in frustration and turn to face Vicky, my

work bestie and fellow romance fiend. "I don't know. I think I had too much to drink last night."

It elicits a chuckle. "Oh, honey… I thought you didn't drink?"

"I don't. That's the whole problem." I shrug. How did it even happen? Oh yeah, one thing led to another, led to… The most humiliating moment of my entire life. My cheeks and ears burn up in an instant.

"Here, let me deal with these books. Meanwhile, you can tell me all about it." She grabs the handle of the trolley and pushes it away from me. I exhale sharply and follow her lead.

"I…" I tried to get out of my comfort zone, and I crashed and burned at the final hurdle. And now the bartender of my naughty dreams is never going to want to see me again. That's what happened.

"Remember last month, when we all went out?" I ask.

"The White Hart. I remember. Because I didn't drink so much that it affected my memory," she teases.

"Right, so… The guy tending bar that night…" I start. Ugh. I don't know how to tell her. And my throat is suddenly so parched, my voice sounds thin as well.

"Ohhh, yes I remember him! Looked like a well-groomed mountain man or lumberjack. His margaritas were to die for. Did you decide to go back and sample his talents again?"

I give her a suspicious glare, but if she's even aware of the innuendo in her words, she hides it well. "I went there last night, yeah."

"Cool, then what happened?" Her tone is light and airy. A little too light…

I try to clear my throat, but it goes horribly wrong and I end up with a coughing fit. Vicky's hand rests on my arm. "Oh dear. Let's get you some water, huh? Have you eaten anything this morning?"

I shake my head, but I can't get a word out yet. I don't even know why I'm refusing. I'm so thirsty, I could kill for a drop of water.

Vicky vanishes for a few moments, before coming back with the water bottle I left at the front desk, and a sandwich, probably her lunch. "Here."

"Thanks," I croak.

A few sips later, my throat has calmed down somewhat. At least I no longer feel like I'm choking on my own breath. And this little interval has also allowed me to come up with a story to answer her questions.

"Right, so I went there for a little change of scenery… Friday night and all that."

Vicky suppresses a smile. "Go on."

"Like, I can't just stay single my whole life, right? It's not like one of my favorite book boyfriends is suddenly going to jump off the page and sweep me off my feet while I'm at home eating ice cream in my pajamas."

"Right..." She gestures at me to carry on, having abandoned the trolley of books next to the Cookbooks section.

"Well, one thing led to another, and he's making me some fancy Cuban cocktail I've never heard of. And then another. And another… Oh god, my head."

"Do you need a p-" Vicky says.

"I already took paracetamol before coming in."

"Okay, good."

"So, I tried to flirt with him." I make a face. "Since, you know, I found him kinda cute last time we were there." As well as every other time I've gone there by myself since then… Which was at least twice a week.

"And it didn't go well?" she asks. Her eyes are wide with anticipation.

This is a dumb idea. I shouldn't share any more. I'm at work, for heaven's sake! And I already know what a massive idiot I've been without having to relive the experience by telling her.

"Yeah," I mumble. "No, it didn't."

"That's okay, though? There are other fish in the sea," Vicky says, patting me on my arm encouragingly. "If you're serious about dating, I can help you set up a profile on some apps. It might be easier if first contact is in writing, what do you think? Weed out the creeps; build up a bit of rapport, then meet somewhere for coffee, maybe. It'll be lower stakes and less nerve wracking."

"Mhm." Other fish in the sea? Not for me, there aren't. For me there's just one: BB. Except those book boyfriends I referred to earlier, he's the only man I've ever pursued. The only man I've ever fantasized about. And embarrassingly, also the guy I've essentially stalked for weeks on end.

He's it. And I messed things up so perfectly, there's no coming back from it.

And to think, he seemed interested in me, too! I don't even know for sure what happened. One moment, everything was great. I felt a high I'd never experienced before. Maybe it was the buzz, or the music playing in the background, or the sheer craziness of the situation I'd gotten myself in. Spoiler alert: It wasn't any of that. It was the man himself. He's sex on legs.

And then… Then, I felt how aroused *he* was. I mean, fair enough, I was pretty much soaking through my jeans at that point as well. And… And it all came flooding back.

How I felt when *it* happened when I was just a teenager. All those judgmental words I heard afterwards. I was being too easy. I was asking for trouble. I was acting like… A… Whore.

That's the word. It makes me sick to even *think* it.

Because slut shaming and victim blaming are not okay. I wouldn't dream of judging another woman like this. If Vicky told me she had a one night stand last night, I wouldn't bat an eye. So, why do I continue to do this to myself? It makes no sense at all.

"He said he'd noticed me, too…" I mumble absentmindedly.

"Did he? He remembered you from last month?" Vicky asks.

"I…" I should shut up now. "I guess so."

She frowns and shakes her head. "Well, but if you guys didn't gel, you didn't gel. Nothing much you can do about it now."

"Mhm." I press the water bottle against one eyelid, and then the other. It's pleasantly cool.

"Okay, so this is entirely normal. You dust yourself off, and you go back out there, and you try again. You can't expect to score if you don't at least try to kick a few balls. Pun not intended. And please don't actually kick anyone in the balls unless they deserve it."

"A football reference? Seriously, Vicky? Have you been reading too many sports romances lately?" I tease.

"As long as it fits." She shrugs.

"Sure. Okay."

"He wasn't even *that* cute, plus he seemed a bit too full of himself. Guys like that are always bad news. You can do way better," she adds. "Trust me. Sometimes you have to kiss a few frogs before you meet your dream man."

I make a face. Yeah, my dream man is right there at the White Hart, making delicious cocktails every night. I was so close to everything I've ever desired, I could almost taste it.

In fact, I did taste him. His lips. Oh my god, his lips were so utterly perfect, the memory of how they felt could make me ugly cry. I'll probably do that tonight. Put on something fitting like *Bridget Jones's Diary* and dribble salty tears into a pint of praline swirl ice cream. I'm pathetic.

"Now," Vicky orders. "Eat the sandwich. You look like you're about to faint."

I make a face and shake my head. "I'm not going to faint from skipping one meal. I've got plenty of reserves."

"I'm not taking no for an answer. Eat a bite."

I sigh and unwrap the sandwich. "I'll just have this much," I tell her while tearing off two bites' worth. "Or, on top of everything else, I'll feel guilty for stealing your lunch."

"It's just a ham sandwich. I'd much rather get a tuna melt from Alice's café later."

Caffeine. That's what my poor throbbing head needs.

"Excellent. It'll be on me," I tell her.

She wraps her arm around my shoulders and pulls me against her. "Trust me. You'll feel better once you get some food in you. And we'll figure out your dating situation in time as well, okay?"

CHAPTER FIVE

*** Nathan ***

My shift starts at four, but I'm antsy about it hours early. I enjoy my work, usually. It appeals to the extrovert in me. I like being surrounded by people every evening, doing my little part in ensuring they have a good time. That's why office jobs never attracted me. I can't imagine sitting in a bland cubicle somewhere, staring at a computer screen all day.

No, I love the ambience at the White Hart. With its warm wood clad interior, and rustically charming furniture. And it's so close to home, I got really lucky they had an opening when I first joined. And seeing *her* there a few times a week has been the icing on the cake for me.

Except today. Today I dread it. Firstly, I have to survive the 'little chat' Dean threatened me with last night. But also just existing in that space, with last night's memories hanging over me like the blade on a guillotine, is going to be a challenge.

After trying and failing to find which way she went when she ran out on me last night, I was awake until the early morning hours trying to analyze what everything meant. I'm torn fifty-fifty between concluding that her flirtation with me was part of a bet or a prank, or else that she was just lonely and I was a convenient target, since there were no other single guys around. Except Frank, the regular who always sits at the far end of the bar looking so grumpy, no-one in their right mind would ever approach him.

This theory made some sense, because she never brought company beyond that first visit, and never spoke to anyone at the pub either except to order her drinks.

Either way, when things got real, she couldn't do it. She didn't want me like that. There was something about me-my body, perhaps-which put her off. Three guesses what that might have been? It all fell apart when we got close, *real* close, so what else am I supposed to think? Maybe those cute glasses of hers need an update, and she just hadn't taken a good look at me earlier? Or she had and she thought she could get past it, but then…

And I know that these conclusions are unhelpful, and are just another way for me to torture myself. This situation would be best resolved with clear communication; perhaps there's an explanation I haven't thought of. But she'd gone without a trace, and I can't seem to fill in her point of view without falling back on my lingering insecurities.

I don't deserve a woman like her. I know I don't. I knew it from the moment I first saw her last month, right up to the second I kissed her. I still know it this morning, as well as every time I remember the taste of her sweet lips. I'm average at best whereas she's exceptional.

But all that doesn't seem to matter to my subconscious, because that part of me is hopelessly obsessed; has been for weeks. I just have to close my eyes to see her again. And the dreams! The dreams are unbearable now, the day after the night before. Because in those, last night didn't happen the same way. Instead, we're still doing everything that *didn't* happen in reality. And it's not just sex, although yes, the imaginary sex is the best I've ever had. It's everything else. It's knowing that I'm hers and she's mine, and nothing could ever come between us. That's what I used to love dreaming about the most.

Fuck.

All is lost. I'm never going to see her again.

It's just after twelve when I can't stand it anymore. I need to get out of here, get some fresh air, and find something else to occupy me before I lose my mind, or worse still, start smoking again.

When I lock up behind me and feel the cold wind hitting my face outside, I know there's only one place to go on my way into work. The same place I always visit, just usually a few hours later: 'Coffee to the Rescue'.

Maybe today I'll skip the double espresso shot and treat myself to something a little extra. Something sugary and decadent and completely incompatible with the healthy lifestyle I've tried to adopt for the past year. It's a poor consolation for my current emotional state. Ugh. This is why she ran last night. Because I don't have the willpower and dedication to live up to her standards.

I bury my hands deep in my coat pockets while making my way through the drizzle and cold. It's late October and the weather matches the season, as well as my mood. Luckily I don't have a long walk ahead of me. By the time I arrive and push open the door to my favorite café, my hair is damp, but not yet wet.

The door chimes, alerting Alice, who runs this place, to my presence. As soon as I enter, the familiar scent of freshly ground coffee beans hits my lungs. So good. This was the right decision after all.

"Hey, Nathan! You're early today. I'll be with you in a sec," Alice greets me.

I give her a little wave. "Hey! Take your time. As you said, I'm early, so there's no need to rush."

She turns around to operate the large and complicated-looking coffee machine before handing a tray of takeaway cups to the elegantly dressed woman waiting ahead of me at the counter. "Hope you enjoy your coffee, and have a nice day!"

I don't pay her or the other customers much attention, that's how preoccupied I am with the contents of the display case in front of me. I didn't plan on ordering any food, but now that I'm here…

"The caramel swirl brownies look amazing, are they new?" I mumble.

Alice smiles at me across the top of the glass case. "They are, indeed."

"Okay, so I'll have one of them for sure, and a double espresso." There. At least I stuck to a healthier drink.

"Takeaway?" she asks.

I shake my head. "Not today."

"Just a minute!" Alice announces before carefully picking up a brownie using a pair of vintage silver tongs and popping it on a porcelain plate. It looks even better up close.

While she brews my coffee, I scan the interior of the café. There's a seat free in the corner facing the windows. I occupy it with my damp coat before making my way back to Alice, who now has the rest of my order ready.

"Do let me know what you think, okay? I need to decide if I'm going to keep these brownies as part of my regular menu, or stick to just the normal ones." She smiles brightly at me while sliding the tray with my order across the counter. And my aching heart feels a little lighter. Just a little.

I take a seat and am about to eat the first bite of brownie when I freeze. From the corner of my eye, a familiar presence walks past the glass front of the café. I can't believe it. It's *her*. The same burgundy-colored overcoat she wore last night. The same dark blonde hair and red glasses.

She pauses in front of the door to retract her umbrella and… She's coming in.

I panic and try to sink down into my chair, which is of course completely pointless. The chair is rather small and I'm too big, so I must look ridiculous.

"Jane and Vicky! So lovely to see you both!" Alice's clear voice chirps above the ambient noise of the café. The two women have their backs turned towards me, allowing me to stare shamelessly at my mystery woman and her curvaceous- God, I'm terrible.

"Well, since Vicky force fed me her lunch sandwich earlier, I figured the least I can do is treat her to something better," she says. Jane. Her name is Jane. And she sounds as chipper today as every other time I've seen her. As if last night didn't affect her at all.

A part of me wants to scream her name and make a scene right here, but a larger part is glad she hasn't turned around yet. I hope she never does, because I wouldn't know what to say anyway.

'Hi, Jane. About last night... We don't really know each other, but you broke my heart. Why?'

That would be laughable. I'm a joke for even considering it.

"I'll have the tuna melt," the other woman says. "And I'm perfectly happy paying for it myself."

"Don't be silly. Two tuna melts, to take away. Do you want anything to drink with that?" Jane turns her head to look in her friend's direction, allowing me a glimpse of her side-profile.

Classically beautiful like a Renaissance painting. There's no doubt it's her. Shit.

I keep as still as possible. I even hold my breath, hoping to blend into the background of the café. Though for a moment, I'm certain she'd be able to hear my heart beat frantically all the way from over here.

"I'll have a cappuccino, or I'll never survive until closing time," Jane says. "Last chance, Vicky."

"Fine. I'll have a chai latte as usual, then," Vicky says.

Alice smiles at the two of them and gets to work preparing their order. Meanwhile, I can't stop staring. What if either of them turns around and catches me gawking? Maybe I should go up there and casually say hello.

But neither of them turns, and nobody catches on

to my shame. And I'm still waffling back and forth between the right thing to do, missing the remaining small talk they share with Alice as she hands them their takeaway order.

And before I know it, they head out the door and I'm still petrified in my seat, afraid to make a move. Deep breaths. They're gone.

Oh shit, she's gone!

I push my seat back and head straight for the counter while shooting hurried glances out the glass door.

"Everything okay with your order? How was that brownie?" Alice asks.

"Uhh, the brownie. Yeah, fine. All good."

She doesn't say anything straight away, but when my gaze meets hers, I find her already looking at me with one hand on her hip and a bemused smile on her face.

"You look like you've just seen a ghost, Nathan."

"Do I? Ah, I think it's sleep deprivation," I mumble.

"Okay… Well, can I get you anything else?"

"I know that woman. The one who just came in. Jane," I say.

"Jane works at the library, so you might have seen her there," Alice suggests.

The library… that's actually perfect.

"She and her friend first visited the White Hart a

few weeks ago. And she's come in by herself a few times since," I explain.

Alice studies my face for a moment before another smile breaks through her calm facade. "You like her."

"Me? Oh, she seems nice and all, but I don't think-"

"It's okay, it can be our little secret," Alice quips. "Under one condition."

"What's that?" I blurt out so fast, I don't even have time to argue the point with her. I already lost my self-respect in front of Jane last night, and Dean, who thinks the worst of me. And by extension his girlfriend, Megan. What does it even matter anymore what anyone thinks?

Alice leans an elbow on the counter, lowering her voice like we're plotting a bank heist.

"You have to tell me what happened last night."

I freeze. "What do you mean?"

"You came in here two hours earlier than normal looking like a sad, lost puppy. Until *she* comes in and rattles you, and now I think she's actually the puppy and suddenly you're no longer lost. Meanwhile, Jane was in a bit of a state herself. If I didn't know any better I'd say she was hungover, or at least flustered, both of which are totally out of character for her. I'm guessing these things aren't mere coincidences."

I run a hand over my jaw, but the scratch of my beard does nothing to soothe me. Hungover?

Flustered? She looked perfect to me. "Nothing happened. Not really."

"Mm-hm." She's not buying it for a second. "So you're saying that my observational instincts have suddenly turned to trash overnight too?"

I let out an involuntary groan. "You're not going to let this go, are you?"

She shakes her head. "I'm only asking because I like you, Nathan, and I want what's best for you. Now, spit it out. Let's see if we can fix whatever is going on with you two."

There's no malice in her tone, and before I know it, I'm talking. "I don't know. She came into the Hart for a drink, as I said. We were talking-flirting, actually-it was going well, I think, and then-" I snap my fingers. "She ran out on me. No explanation. But Dean saw her leave, and he's convinced I did something wrong, so he's waiting to tear me a new one before my shift today. He's just paranoid after that whole disaster with Megan's friend, Sam, earlier in the year, because I swear I didn't-"

"Hey, hey, hey," Alice says gently. "If everything went exactly as you say it did, perhaps there's some other explanation. Look, you seem to really like her, and she works at the library, so maybe you should just… I don't know… go borrow a book."

"Borrow a book," I repeat, like it's the most ludicrous suggestion in the world.

"Yeah, people do it all the time," she deadpans. "And it might be easier than staring at her back while she orders coffee, until she telepathically gets your number."

I let out a short laugh despite myself. "I don't want to weird her out."

"Then don't," Alice says simply. "Just be yourself. You've got this. So what if last night ended on a strange note? Everyone deserves a second chance." She winks and moves to wipe down the espresso machine, clearly done with the topic.

But the seed is planted. The library. A second chance. I can do that.

Maybe I should do that right now, before Dean murders me and I never get the opportunity.

CHAPTER SIX

*** Jane ***

The afternoon crawls only slightly faster than the morning did. But at least the cappuccino and tuna melt Vicky insisted on for lunch have helped settle my stomach.

I'm most of the way through the giant stack of cookbooks Vicky abandoned in the aisle before lunch when I catch a glimpse of someone approaching the counter.

Holy shit. It's him! My knees threaten to buckle underneath me when he looks up just in time to find me gaping at him. God, kill me now.

And what the hell is he doing here?

Vicky spots him at exactly that moment. Her back straightens and she puts on her cheerful customer service voice.

"Hey there, how can I help you?"

BB doesn't say anything at first; he's still too preoccupied looking at me. It's so damn obvious. Vicky picks up on it immediately and turns around. She smiles at me and mouths the words 'it's okay.'

Is it? Is it okay? I don't think so. None of this is okay. I'm not ready.

"Uhh, I was wondering about getting a library card," BB says.

"Is that so? You like to read, do you?" Although I can only see her back from where I'm standing, I can *hear* her fake smile through her words. She's being prickly on purpose. Why? As mortified as I am standing face-to-face with the man of my dreams again, I'm also… Well, the way he looks at me isn't all bad. It's almost apologetic.

I force myself into action and cross the distance between myself and the reception desk in record time.

"A library card. We can do that, can't we, Vicky?" I urge.

She turns to me with one eyebrow raised.

"I mean… it's all part of the job," she mumbles.

"Be a dear and fetch one of those forms. You know. The library card application forms."

She frowns and reaches into the drawer underneath her desk.

"No, those are the old ones. We need the *new* forms," I insist. "The ones in the back."

"Oh! Yes, they're in the back. Silly me." She frowns at me again.

Vicky walks away and disappears through the staff door, and I just try to breathe.

Big Bartender smiles subtly. "Do you always send

your coworkers on scavenger hunts for paperwork that's right there already?"

"Only when I need a moment to-uh-make sure everything's in order," I say, which sounds so much more suspicious out loud than it did in my head.

He leans an elbow on the counter, lowering his voice. "I just… wanted to see you again. After last night. Wanted to make sure you're okay."

There's a little lurch in my stomach at his words. I open my mouth to confirm that I'm indeed okay, but my throat decides to close up on me instead. Because I'm not. I'm falling apart again.

He glances over his shoulder toward the stacks, as if checking we're still alone, and then slides a small folded scrap of paper across the counter. "My number. In case you feel like… talking. Or seeing each other. Or to give me a chance to apologize for whatever I did wrong. No pressure."

My fingers brush the paper, and it's warm from his pocket.

"Thanks," I squeak.

Wait, did he say apologize? If anyone has anything to be sorry for, it's me. He was perfect. He *is* perfect.

Just then, Vicky returns with a stack of the exact same forms that are in the drawer between BB and me. Her eyes flit from the paper in my hand to his face like she's observing a drug deal. My cheeks heat up instantly until I glow from ear to ear and my heart races so hard, I'm definitely moments away from fainting.

"All set," she says brightly, but the brightness has that sharp edge to it. "Let's get you signed up."

"Cool, so, I gotta-" I gesture to the trolley I left in the aisle behind Vicky and me.

"Back to work, I get it," he says, shooting a brief smile my way. "Nice to see you again, Jane."

"Yeah… Nice," I mumble before rushing off.

God, I feel stupid. Unprepared and out of sorts. Last night, somehow the stars aligned for me and I knew exactly what to say to him. At least for a while, until we were actually alone. But just now, with Vicky scrutinizing every exchange, I behaved even worse than my usual awkward self. And still, I have the note with his phone number burning a hole in my pocket. And a strange warmth in the center of my chest inspired by that last little smile he directed at me before I ran.

I didn't just run. I ran and hid. And I'm still hiding fifteen minutes later when I watch him head back out through the glass doors from behind the children's picture book display diagonally across from the reception desk.

"It's safe," Vicky calls out. "You can come out now."

I try to shake off the lingering anxiety and force myself to face her.

"I'm sorry," I stammer. "I'm sorry for palming him off on you."

"I am on desk duty. That is literally my job." Vicky folds her arms and stares me down. "You sure you're okay with him just showing up here?"

I shrug, hopefully nonchalantly. "It's fine. You heard him; he just wanted a library card. It's a *public* library, after all."

Her silence is heavy, and I know exactly what she's thinking: that whatever I told her about last night wasn't the whole truth. And she'd be right. I left a lot of stuff out.

"Yeah, he just wanted a library card," she repeats. "He just woke up this morning and thought to himself that he needed to get himself a library card. Out of the blue. Life sure is funny sometimes. Did you tell him you worked here?"

"Very funny," I repeat, ignoring her question. She's not buying any of this. Even I don't. He was looking for me. That's why he had that note ready to hand to me. She's my friend, and I love that she tries to engage, but she doesn't need to know everything. Certainly not that I never told him I worked here, actually, so he somehow tracked me down on his own. I don't know whether to be flattered or concerned.

Seeing my dream guy again today was a shocker, but also... Having him here like this... in a safe, normal setting, surrounded by books and bad fluorescent lighting, was nothing like last night. And I kind of love that. I kind of love him for handing me that note, which I still haven't dared to look at and probably won't until I get home. Or until I lock myself in the bathroom, far away from Vicky's prying eyes.

"Let's finish tidying away this final stack of returns and call it a day, what do you say?" I suggest.

"Mhm," Vicky grunts. "Let's do that."

*** Nathan ***

I reach the White Hart half an hour before my usual shift, with a growing sense of dread hanging over me. Although after last night, and then my impromptu visit to the library to see Jane again, I'd much rather crawl back into bed and forget today ever happened, but I still have a job to do. For now.

I promised that I'd finish up whatever work I left undone last night. It's the weekend, and as such, there are already some punters dotted around the pub, but the real rush won't start until later. I'm halfway through preparing a list of stuff we need to reorder, when a dark cloud appears in front of the open doorway to the storeroom.

"A word, Nathan," Dean's voice is low and threatening. Just as I couldn't possibly forget last night, neither did he.

"Sure thing, Dean." I sigh and put my tablet down, ready to face my one-Hulk firing squad.

"Last night wasn't okay. After what happened to Sam at the comedy night in April, the last thing the boss needs is another controversy, you get me?"

I nod. "Absolutely. That was a disgrace that should have never happened."

"Glad we're in agreement. Now, care to explain why one of our newest repeat customers ran out of here in tears last night after closing?" Dean asks.

I sigh and shake my head. If only I knew. "She ordered her drink from me once Alexis went upstairs and we got talking. There really wasn't much else to it. We started talking and we got along, and she agreed to stay back after closing so we could..." I can't quite finish that sentence.

"So you could-what?"

"Get to know each other better... You know. We seemed to get along great. She was interested, I was definitely-"

"We have CCTV, you guys," a female voice speaks up behind Dean. Alexis. Bloody great. Now it's two against one.

"Right, we have CCTV," I confirm. "Which no doubt you've already reviewed."

Dean steps aside, allowing me out of the store, only to be met by Alexis with her hands propped up on her hips and a stern expression on her face. Then again, that's pretty much her normal expression, anyway.

"When Dean expressed his concern about certain events from last night, I didn't have much choice."

"Great." I sigh and shake my head. So she already watched my fall from grace. "And did you see anything of concern?"

"The two of you looked awfully cozy together after closing. Until suddenly."

I straighten myself. Since I've already lost every last bit of my self-respect, I might as well make the most of the situation.

"No, honestly, Alexis. I'm grasping at fucking straws. Everything was going *really* well. She was interested. She even made the first fucking move. And then... What the hell happened? I have no clue. I just know that we kissed, and then she bolted like she'd-"

Alexis shakes her head and scrutinizes me top to bottom.

"I can only conclude that... Reality didn't quite live up to her-" I glance down at myself.

Dean continues to glare at me silently, and Alexis... She's chewing her bottom lip in frustration.

"You've never given me cause for concern before," Alexis remarks.

I sigh.

"I wish I could just have a quiet conversation with

her. Not to pressure her, but just to understand where things went wrong, you know?" I ask. "Because I certainly never want to be in the same situation again."

Alexis nods silently, while Dean looks unfazed.

"Okay, Dean, looks like it's getting busier out there. You're needed at the door."

I exhale and find my shoulders slumping just a little more than I'd like. This isn't me. This isn't who I want to be at all. I gave it my best shot, I even handed her my number at the library before shift. And now the ball is in her court. Jane… my mystery woman. Although clearly I'm not it for her.

"I've got my eye on you," Dean threatens.

I nod in silence.

"I'm really sorry, Alexis. If it makes you feel better, I can dust off my resume and look for something-" I say.

"Absolutely not. I'd like to think you're a good guy, Nathan. We don't have any rules against fraternizing with customers after hours. I mean that's how Dean and Megan started off last year. But maybe it would be better to be a little cautious going forward, if you know what I mean."

I keep my hands up in defense. "Yeah, fine. Whatever you say."

"Now, chin up. We've got a busy night ahead and I can't have our friendly neighborhood bartender sulking over some woman who doesn't know her own mind."

"I'm not sulking!" And Jane isn't just *some ignorant woman!* She's… sensitive, maybe? Wait, did Alexis just make a Spiderman reference? That's so out of character, it's actually kind of funny.

"Tell your face that. No offense," she fires back.

I press my lips together tightly to stop myself from arguing. But the twinkle in Alexis' eye stops that impulse dead. She can be abrasive, but she did get Dean out of my hair and that's a great sign. I've done all I can, just as I did with Jane at the library. I'm all out of moves. And despite everything, I haven't lost my optimism completely. Who knows, this whole situation might still work itself out, or at least I might find out what got Jane so spooked last night. So, I take Alexis' words to heart, dust myself off and take my position behind the bar with a little smile to mask my lingering confusion.

CHAPTER SEVEN

*** Jane ***

I always enjoy my quiet Sundays in. After five-and-a-half days of socializing at work, I always look forward to getting some solitude. Curled up on the couch with a good novel, I love to while away the hours until my social battery is charged and I'm ready to face the reading public again on Monday.

But not this Sunday. This Sunday, I can't seem to get into my latest super steamy boss/employee BDSM romance. Every time the action on the page heats up, the characters start swimming in front of my eyes, interspersed with glimpses of my kiss with Nathan at the White Hart.

Nathan.

That's his name. I know now, because it said so on the little note he slipped me with his phone number that I've studied about a million times. I've looked at it, gripped it tightly against my chest, even smelled it, before hiding it away in my journal after penning every detail of our second encounter.

But, have I actually done anything with the

information? Have I picked up the phone, dialed his number, and been proactive? No, I haven't. I'm not ready. Or am I?

As much as I beat myself up yesterday morning at work, thinking I'd thrown away my one chance with him, I'm not quite ready to consider the opposite. But him turning up at the library meant that all was not lost. And honestly? It was nice-more than nice-to see him somewhere calm, with no blaring music or tipsy shouting in the background.

In the harsh library light, without the haze of Cuban rum, I could notice little things I'd missed before: the way his hair curled slightly at the nape, the faint dimple in his beard when he smiled, the way his voice sounded so warm and disarming but still bassy enough to have a mysterious edge. He didn't push, didn't corner me-just handed me the note like it was the most natural thing in the world. No pressure. Just… an opening.

And maybe that's what threw me off more than anything-because low stakes are somehow scarier than high ones. In the pub, I could chalk everything up to alcohol and noise and the thrill of the moment. But now? Now it's quiet, and I still want to say yes. And it seems, so does he.

I guess he was serious about wanting the chance to get to know me. Why else did he bother to seek me out? That's all I've ever wanted. Well, okay, I wanted the filthy encounter in the pub's storeroom too, but I also want *more.* It was all too much for me at the moment. And it was my own shame that sent me running yet again yesterday while Vicky got him signed up for his library card.

But maybe… it doesn't have to be that way. Maybe I can learn to stay put.

I wish I knew how to approach this. Calling him is out of the question, obviously. But a text… Maybe I could send him a text? I'm tempted to talk it through with Vicky, but in my eagerness to get her off my back yesterday, I didn't even talk to her about the note.

Ugh.

Social conventions are hard. I don't even know why she puts up with me. She's so open and worldly, and I'm so much more reserved, bordering on secretive. As long as we talk about books, it's all good. We have so much in common. But I've never shared my true self with anyone.

She's my best friend. My only friend. And I've made damn sure she knows only the bare minimum about me. Only the surface level stuff. I guess that's the answer, then. Before I reach out to Nathan, I need to make sure I have at least one person in my corner. Vicky is the obvious choice, no matter how awkward and icky it feels.

I put my book down on the sofa and reach for my

phone instead. I can call *her* without getting a panic attack. Here goes nothing.

"Hey, Jane!" Vicky's cheerful voice almost startles me. That was quick. As if she was waiting for a call.

"Vicky, hope I'm not disturbing your Sunday." My heart is already fluttering and I haven't even said anything yet. A part of me considers ending the call with a lame excuse already.

"Not at all, what's up?" she asks.

I take a deep breath. No chickening out this time. If I can't tell my one and only friend about literally the most monumental thing that's happened to me in years, then what hope is there for me?

"So… I need to tell you something. And apologize. Mostly apologize." I close my eyes, imagining Vicky's thoughtful expression.

"That sounds awfully dramatic, what's going on?"

"It's about-" I have to stop myself from calling him BB out loud. "-Nathan," I say.

"Library card Nathan," she answers.

"Right. I haven't been entirely honest with you. I'm really sorry." My palms are sweaty, so I try to wipe them off on my pajama bottoms. To no avail.

"It's fine. You don't owe me anything you're not ready to share." I almost hear her shrugging at her end. Or maybe I'm just imagining it because it feels comforting.

"We made out. At the pub, after closing. We were

going to have a one night stand. It was going *super* well, actually," I blurt out, and then I wait, my heart hammering in my chest.

She exhales sharply. "But you said- nevermind. I'm not here to judge. So why were you so broken up about him the next morning, did he do something? Did he mistreat you?"

"Ohh! No, not at all, he was utterly perfect!" I complain.

There's another pause on the line. "So… if he was so perfect, why did you look like you'd been hit by a bus the next day?" she asks.

I fiddle with the seam of the couch cushion. "Because… I, um. I didn't exactly… stick around."

"What?" Vicky asks.

"I… sort of… left."

"Like, left while he was asleep? Or, what do you mean?"

"As in, I fled," I say, cringing at my own voice. "We were still making out, and I freaked, and I fucking ran."

"Jane. You ghosted him mid-kiss?"

"Not-well-kind of. But it wasn't like that. It was just-" I bite my lip, unsure how much to say.

"It was just…?" she prompts.

I lean my head back against the sofa and shut my eyes. "We were still at the pub. We'd just had our first kiss, and things were heating up and I got… this feeling. Like I shouldn't be there. Like I'd made some kind of horrible mistake, except I hadn't. He was… lovely. God, it was so hot, too. Everything I'd hoped for. And then, out of nowhere, I had these thoughts."

"Thoughts?"

"Just dumb stuff my mom used to say." The words taste bitter. "About girls who… you know. About how you shouldn't get carried away. That it's… cheap."

"Oh, Jane…"

"I know. It's stupid. But once it started, I couldn't shut it off. I couldn't breathe. I just had to… get out."

She's quiet for a second, and I feel her rearranging her opinion of the whole situation in real time. "So, basically, you didn't run because you didn't like him. You ran because of… voices in your head."

"I guess," I mumble. "I told myself I'd messed it all up, because despite everything, I'm still-" I stop, the word *broken* just sitting there on the tip of my tongue. "-still me."

"Well," Vicky says slowly, "that explains why you were all doom-and-gloom the next day. But it doesn't explain how he ended up at the library yesterday, staring at you like a lovesick puppy. Just applying for a library card, my ass. Did you tell him where you worked? Is that why he showed up?"

I pinch the bridge of my nose. "Yeah. No, we hadn't exactly… talked. But you were right. The library card thing was just an excuse. He came to hand me a note with his phone number. And I keep staring at it, freaking out all over again, while also really wanting to text him. I just don't know..."

"Jane, Jane, Jane... Let's take a breath for a moment and look at the facts. You made out with this guy at the pub after closing, and you wanted to do a whole lot more than that, correct?"

My throat feels so tight it's hard to get a word out. "Yep."

"And instead of going through with it, you panicked mid-kiss and ran out on him. And he *somehow* tracked you down to the library yesterday to give you his number, even though you never told him where you worked. And then, instead of taking his application after you sent me away, you kind of ran away in the middle of that too, didn't you?" she asks.

"Yep."

"And now you want to call him, because you're still hung up on him and feel like you made a mistake on Friday night? But you're also scared and don't know how to approach it."

"Pretty much." I breathe a sigh of relief, feeling kind of warm and comforted by the fact that she seems to understand exactly what's going on.

"You're not going to want to hear this, but I think you maybe need to listen to your intuition. There's something about this guy which rubs you the wrong way. That's why you ran on Friday, and you ran yesterday, and despite having his phone number since yesterday, you still haven't reached out to him."

Wait, what? "No, that's not-"

"Think about it, Jane. So, you kissed on Friday night. And for all *he* knows, you had second thoughts and ran out on the whole situation. Still, he somehow found out where you work, despite not knowing anything about you because apparently you guys didn't really talk before getting handsy. And he decided to just turn up at your workplace for what, a redo of your hookup? I know this all seems terribly romantic if it's in a novel, but this is the real world. And it's giving serious red flags."

I press my lips together and swallow the barrage of arguments that my brain already throws my way. Maybe it was a mistake to tell Vicky the truth. She's twisting things completely out of shape. Teddington is a small place. Maybe he saw me at the library before? Who knows how he knew where to find me. The fact is, I'm glad to get a second chance with him but she's intent on crushing that idea.

"Okay," I say instead.

"I think you dodged a bullet, Jane. As I told you yesterday, you can do much better than this guy. Now, after knowing the truth, I'm even more convinced of that."

I sigh and shake my head. Then why does it still feel like it's now or never? I've never so much as gone on a date before! The only relationship awareness I have is whatever I've read about in books. Not that I'd admit that out loud to anyone, least of all Vicky.

But after years of living my wildest fantasies only in my own daydreams, I finally had something real. For however short it lasted. And this guy is *still interested*. He made an effort to approach me again. That has to mean something. And I don't think it's what Vicky is reading into it.

"You'll be okay, Jane. Try not to take this to heart. We all have lapses in judgement and make mistakes sometimes," she says.

"Okay," I repeat, while staring off into the distance. "Thanks. I'm gonna go eat ice cream and watch a sad movie."

"Great idea. If you want company, shall I come over?"

"No!" I snap before catching myself. "I mean, no, thank you. I think I need to think about everything alone." How is it that my palms are still clammy despite me obsessively wiping them off throughout this phone call? Ugh!

"No worries. Thanks for telling me everything. I know it was hard for you to share."

I smile half-heartedly at my phone while blinking an errant tear away. "Thanks for being there for me,

Vicky."

"Ah, stop it. Go on, enjoy your ice cream and your movie. This too shall pass. I'll see you at work tomorrow."

"Okay, bye." I hang up and throw the phone all the way to the other side of the sofa.

Well, that didn't help. Earlier, I was just anxious about how to approach Nathan. Now I doubt Vicky, the only friend I have, while also doubting myself and Nathan's motives, as well as everything else. I can't function like this. I slump back against the sofa cushions, pick up the remote and switch on the first thing that appears. But I don't really watch. Instead, I try to process everything that's happened, along with everything that hasn't (yet), and all the mess in between.

I mindlessly pick up my journal and dump all my conflicting thoughts out onto the page.

Vicky was right about one thing. I have to look at the facts and trust my intuition. And the fact is, she wasn't exactly being objective, either.

By the time I stop and read what I just wrote down, I see it's not so much about my doubts or her suspicions, but more confirmation that my heart knows exactly what it wants. And… It's still him.

CHAPTER EIGHT

*** Nathan ***

I didn't expect Jane to reach out to me on Saturday itself. I didn't even really expect her to call on Sunday. I had my secret hopes, but whatever.

A part of me wondered whether she'd want to get in touch at all. I don't even know this girl, and she has me all twisted up inside. I could be romantic and attach some grand meaning to that, or I could be practical and put it down to the confusing hot and cold signals she puts out. First, on Friday night at the pub. She was all in, until she wasn't. Then, on Saturday at the library, she got rid of her colleague, allowing us a brief moment alone. That signaled interest. And then as soon as the colleague came back, she bolted, as though she couldn't get away from me quickly enough. If not for the apologetic look in her eye when she did.

Of course I'm hooked! She's a mystery I just can't unravel.

And then, there's everything that came before. She visited the Hart for weeks on her own, only to do everything in her power to avoid me. If Friday hadn't happened, I would have continued to attach a different meaning to her behavior. But then, she kept coming back. If I'd made her so uncomfortable, she could have simply gone to one of the other pubs in town. Teddington isn't huge, but there are at least half a dozen decent options around.

She was there for me. That's why she was always already looking in my direction whenever I shot a glance her way. That's why she kept coming back, and also why she avoids me so hard. But now that the spell between us is broken.

It's Monday morning, my regular day off, and despite having had another rough, sleepless night, I'm almost tempted to go into the Hart anyway, just to see if she'll show up at night. And anyway, sitting here obsessing over everything doesn't help my mental state.

I'm still waffling between staying in and finishing the latest Ryan Holiday book I started, or heading into work for an impromptu extra shift, when my phone dings with a notification that makes my decision for me.

It's a simple 'Hi' from a number that isn't in my contact list. Now, it could be a scammer, but… she's still typing. And I save her as 'Jane' without giving it a second thought. It has to be.

I stare at the screen, thumb hovering, watching the

little bubble pulse as she types.

I half expect the next message to be something equally minimal, something that leaves me wondering if she's about to tell me to leave her the hell alone.

Finally, it comes through:

It's Jane. From the library. And the pub. Obviously.

I grin despite myself. "Obviously," I mutter to my empty flat.

I tap out a reply:

Hey. I was worried I'd overstepped on Saturday, showing up at your work.

The typing bubble appears, vanishes, and comes back. She's hesitating. I picture her curled up in an armchair somewhere, overthinking every word, and it makes me want to tell her she doesn't need to. Just tell me how it is. I can take it, however this thing turns out.

Sorry about running off on you, she sends at last. *On Friday night, as well as Saturday. I… tend to do that. Run off.*

That gets my full attention. I lean back on the sofa, thumb poised over the keyboard.

Okay… I'm sorry if I did anything to make you uncomfortable.

Another long pause. I'm about to put the phone down when the bubble blinks again.

I meant what I said. About me being the problem. I didn't want you to think I wasn't interested.

Something in my chest loosens.

Good. Because I definitely am. I hit send before I can talk myself out of it. *Interested, I mean. In seeing you again.*

The bubble appears almost instantly this time and shocks me even more than whatever came before.

How about coffee?

I all but swallow my own breath. A coffee date? Excellent! This is already going much better than I dared to hope. Before I know it, I find myself tapping out an overly eager response.

Today is my day off, so I'm free all day. Let me know the time and place and I'll be there. It'll probably be better to continue this conversation in person anyway.

That sends her into a retreat of sorts. Typing, not typing, hesitating, and likely agonizing. It's like I observed earlier. Hot and cold. In and out. She's clearly in turmoil, and it's spilling over into our interactions. I wish I knew what the hang-up was. Maybe I could help somehow. Finally, another message.

Do you know the little café on the High Street? I could duck out of work during my lunch hour…

I find my cheeks heating up, even though no one's watching. As much as I loved the idea of meeting over coffee, I hate that Alice would watch the two of us try to figure this out. Not when it's this fragile and fresh. I try to come up with something clever as a counter proposal.

Coffee to the Rescue? I know it… But… If it's lunch you're after, we could grab some proper food somewhere else instead? My treat.

My relief at having come up with a plausible reason to switch location is short lived. Because after a few seconds of her typing, she stops. And then… Nothing.

*** Jane ***

I hurriedly put my phone away as soon as I spot Vicky turning the corner around the children's book display. So much for my little moment of privacy.

"Oh, there you are! If I didn't know any better, I'd think you've been avoiding me today," she teases.

Guilt fills my chest instantly. Despite her light tone, she's absolutely correct. I have avoided her. But I can't very well tell her that without opening myself up to too many prying questions.

"No, why would you think that?" I ask.

"The fact that you've barely spoken to me when you came in today and have made exactly zero progress on this stack of biographies in the past half hour? But maybe I'm reading too much into things." Vicky shrugs and shoots a curious glance at me. "You're okay, right? I just want to know if you're okay."

"I'm okay." I blow an errant lock of hair out of my face. "I just haven't slept very well. All that ice cream

I ate yesterday did a number on my digestive system."

"Uh-huh." Vicky shakes her head. "He's really not worth it, you know? Not worth this amount of stress."

"Oh, this isn't about Nathan!" I interject.

"Ah yes, his name is Nathan. I forgot." She eyes me suspiciously. "What do you say we grab one of those tuna melts for lunch again?"

Crap. Yeah, no that won't work. That won't work at all.

"I really shouldn't. I thought of heading home at lunch instead. I've got some leftover porridge from breakfast which would be much more soothing to my stomach," I lie. Well, sort of. I do have leftover porridge in the fridge, but other than a raging case of anxiety, my stomach is fine.

"I can come with." Vicky smiles brightly. "Do you still have that lovely Lady Grey tea you brought in once?"

Ugh. Now I'm stuck. "Yep, sure. I've still got some, indeed."

"It would be nice to get a little walk in at lunchtime. The weather is rather lovely today. Who knows how many sunny days we'll get before winter rolls in," she explains.

"Yeah…" I try to smile back at her, but it feels more like a grimace. God, now I'm really stuck.

"Okay, well, let's get through the morning first. I'm

going back to the front desk now." Vicky's tone is suspiciously light and airy again, and she walks back where she came from with a spring in her step.

Crappity crap. I fish my phone out of my pocket as soon as she's out of sight and tap out a quick message to Nathan.

Something's come up, and I can't do lunch anymore. How about dinner? You pick the place. I get off at six and then I can meet you there any time after.

Send.

Only when I re-read it after sending do I notice I've written 'get off at six' and I cringe. That particular exchange between us on Friday was especially suggestive. When he said he gets off at midnight, I told him hopefully so will I. Argh. Maybe this was all a mistake.

Cool. There's a lovely French restaurant near the park. How about seven-thirty, does that work?

I try to breathe. Seven-thirty at a fine dining restaurant I would never visit myself. Suddenly the stakes are a whole lot higher than they were when I suggested coffee earlier.

It's time to pull up my big girl pants and be totally honest with him. If I go through with this, I'll have to sit him down and tell him that all that stuff I told him on Friday wasn't really me. I just played a part I had no business playing. Quoting suggestive pick-up lines at him… Jesus. What was I even thinking? If he expects some kind of sex goddess, he's sorely mistaken. Hell, even if he expects someone halfway neurotypical, he's similarly out of luck.

CHAPTER NINE

*** Nathan ***

Seven-thirty approaches fast, and I grow increasingly nervous. For some reason, it feels like there's just so much riding on this one dinner and I don't feel quite like myself anymore.

I'm far from a ladies' man, but this level of anxiety over a first date is new, even to me. I'm the guy who goes with the flow. The one who says 'this is who I am, take it or leave it.'

But not today. Not with her.

I spent way too long getting dressed, and I'm still early. Rather than continuing to pace around the house, I take a round through the park on the way to the restaurant to burn off some of this restless energy.

Why do I even care so much? Jane is beautiful, sure. She's way out of my league, but so what? She reached out to *me* today. And she was the one who upgraded a low stakes coffee to dinner. That has to mean something.

Coffee could have meant she just wanted to talk things through, but dinner can only be interpreted as a date. This is what I craved on Friday night.

I cut through the park one final time, my breath making faint clouds in the crisp evening air. The glow from the old streetlamps shimmers on the damp foot path, and I catch myself checking my watch way too often for comfort.

By the time I reach the restaurant-a cozy little French place tucked between a home furnishing shop and a daycare, both closed for the evening-I'm still ten minutes early. I slow down as I approach, half to catch my breath and half because I want to get my nerves under control.

And then I see her.

She's already here, standing near the entrance, both hands gripping the elegant sling bag hanging in front of her. Her hair is up, neat but with a few loose strands catching the light from the window beside her. Underneath that same signature red overcoat, she's wearing a knitted sweater dress that hugs her in all the right places and knee high boots that somehow make her look both elegant and... dangerous.

It hits me in one dizzying, unguarded moment-this is it. She's it.

The thought is so strong, it almost knocks the air out of me. I've never believed in that instant 'one look and you know' nonsense. Marriage? Settling down? Never been on my mind. But right now, I can't imagine ever wanting to walk away from her.

She turns her head, spots me, and smiles-small at first, then warmer when our eyes lock. Something unravels in my chest.

I walk toward her, suddenly conscious of every step, every movement. My usual easy grin feels… too casual for what I feel.

"Hi," I manage, and my voice comes out raspier than I intended.

Her eyes linger on me for a moment longer than necessary, and I swear, if she asked me to right now, I'd hand over my whole damn heart.

"I've got some things I need to clear up," she says, the words tumbling out fast, like she's rehearsed them. "And if you want to pull the plug after that, that's okay."

The sentence hits me straight in the chest, into that same heart I was ready to serve up on a silver platter just now. Pull the plug? We literally just got here. I keep my expression neutral, though my pulse is doing its own panicked drum solo.

"Okay," I say slowly.

She folds her arms-not defensive, more like she's trying to comfort herself. It's adorable, irresistible. "The stuff at the pub… all those things I said? That wasn't really me. I'm not that kind of girl."

I almost laugh in shock as my heart sinks down into my stomach. She didn't mean it when she flirted with me. Expected, if disappointing. "That's fine. I get it."

"No, really." Her eyes lock on mine, searching for any sign I'm just being polite. "I'm not like that. I was just…" she hesitates, like she can't quite believe she's admitting this, "…playing a role. Trying on a different… me"

Something in me just cracks open. I can't help it- my mouth opens, but I can't quite think of what to say. So… she was acting. Which is fine, like I already said. Expected. What's confusing is that she wrote in her messages that she's interested. That *is* what she wrote, right? I didn't imagine that. But she didn't mean what she said about *how* interested?

She frowns a little, like she's not sure how to proceed.

"Well, I meant what *I* said," I tell her. "About wanting to get to know you."

"Oh, well, me too, obviously," she stammers, which makes me frown. It's noticeable too, because now she's turning red and fidgeting nervously with the chain strap of her bag. "It was more, the presentation… You know?"

I slowly shake my head. "I'm not sure that I do."

"God, how do I explain?" She huffs in frustration. "I don't know how to do all this, and I was pretty nervous, so… I kind of… I quoted some of my favorite romance novel dialogue lines to you. On Friday."

She looks up at me, eyebrows pulled together in concern. And I… I want to say something sensible, and yet when I open my mouth, I can't formulate a single word. So instead, I chuckle. Which then turns into more of a laugh.

Her eyes widen, and for a moment, I fear she's going to tear up. I take a step forward, gently placing my hand on her arm, which makes her wince under her breath and lean in. That gives me the courage I need to continue talking.

"I'm not laughing at you," I explain.

"No?" She nervously shifts her weight from one foot to the other.

"I'm relieved, actually."

She presses her lips together and looks up at me. For a glorious ten seconds, she stares into my eyes and I feel like I can see straight into her soul.

"I'm relieved, because…" I mumble. Because I'm not that kind of guy? Because I didn't want to bend her across the bar counter and have my way with her on Friday? Well no, I definitely wanted all that. A growing part of me still wants it right now. "I think this is better. You, me, a nice quiet meal. Getting to know each other. And then…" I shrug.

"And then…" she repeats under her breath while giving me a stare that can only mean one thing. Maybe she wasn't just acting after all.

Damn it if my body doesn't react instantly. Time

for me to shift my weight from one foot to the other, because things are getting tight down there. I hope it isn't obvious.

"I'm definitely *not* pulling the plug," I clarify.

She breathes a sigh of relief and smiles again. It's that same bright smile she shot my way when she first spotted me, and I melt. Because stupid though it might be, I have that feeling again. That persistent voice in the back of my head telling me this is it. She's it. She's all I want.

"Shall we?" I ask, offering her my arm.

She hesitates for a split second, but then slips her hand into the crook of my elbow and joins me by my side. And I feel like I've already won.

*** Jane ***

Throughout our starters, I feel like I'm floating on a cloud. The restaurant is quaint yet classy. The food is amazing. And Nathan…

He might as well be a god. Outside, I was still in a good mood to run, but when he laughed and told me he preferred to get to know me over dinner… That changed everything for me.

At first, he leads the conversation, asking me about my work at the library, how I got into that job, commenting on how great it must be to be surrounded by books all day. I agree wholeheartedly. It's the perfect job for me, considering I'm such a book worm myself.

He admits to being an avid reader, too. And although he's into vastly different books than I am, he doesn't seem to mind our differences. One glass of wine into the evening, and part of the way through our entrees, he asks me about those romance books I was referring to, which makes me blush yet again.

God, I've blushed and smiled so much already, my cheeks feel tired.

"Ah, they're just… You know. Escapism," I say.

"All fiction is escapism. That's why we love it," he counters. "I think it's amazing how something seemingly bland like letters on a page allow us to enter a different world."

"Or indeed occupy a different character for a while," I add.

"Exactly! It's the closest thing to magic I've ever encountered." He smiles wistfully before adding, "Until now."

It takes me a minute to formulate the next logical question, because somehow he knows exactly what to say to me.

"So you read a lot of fiction, too?" I ask, finally.

"I try to vary my reading, yes. Alongside nonfiction on all sorts of topics, I'm partial to fantasy and sci-fi."

He's obviously passionate about books too, and it makes me smile. And now his 'magic' comment makes sense too, since I'm sure a lot of the books he enjoys probably contain quite a bit of that.

"Maybe that's why you're so good at conversing," I say, half-teasing, half-serious. "You've practiced being other confident people in books."

His grin is quick and disarming. "Maybe. Or maybe I've found the right person I want to talk to."

Heat rushes to my face again, and I take a sip of wine to hide it. The way he says it-so matter-of-factly, like it's not a line, not a trick-makes something flutter wildly inside me.

"You make it sound easy," I murmur.

"It is easy," he says simply, leaning back in his chair. His gaze lingers, steady but not invasive. "With you, anyway."

And just like that, my carefully built defenses wobble again. I fiddle with my fork, anything to break the intensity of his attention. The restaurant hums softly around us-cutlery clinking, low conversation, the occasional burst of laughter from another table. But it all feels far away.

I want to argue. Reiterate, that this… date, this whole whirlwind-it's not me. But here I am, cheeks aching from smiling, heart tripping over itself at every word he says.

"Jane?" His voice is gentle, questioning.

I blink, realizing I've gone silent too long. "Sorry. I was just… thinking."

"About?" He tilts his head slightly, waiting.

I hesitate, but his openness makes it easier to breathe. "About how weird this is."

"Dinner?" he teases lightly, but the hint of a crease between his eyebrows tells me he's not as comfortable as he'd like to be.

"Dates," I admit. I look up to study his face more fully, scanning for any sign of disapproval.

His eyes soften, as do the corners of his mouth. "You don't like to date much?"

I swallow hard and shrug. "I guess I've never really met a guy I wanted to go on a date with, until… you know, now."

For a moment, neither of us moves. Then his smile spreads slowly, lighting his whole face, and I feel it land inside me like sunlight breaking through clouds.

"This may sound really unimaginative, but… I feel the same way." He leans across the table and invites me to place my fingers on his palm.

I can't stop smiling while looking at it. How warm and reassuring his touch feels. But also…

"No way," I mumble. "I've seen you. How you interact with everyone at the White Hart. How effortless you make it look. We're not alike, you and I. You're confident and outspoken, and I…"

He rubs circles on my hand with his thumb, round and round. It's calming and also makes my heart race faster.

"That's just my job. I do it on autopilot, like you organize books all day. And the secret is…"

"Yes?" My voice is barely a whisper above the buzz of conversation around us.

"Ever since you first walked in four weeks ago, I couldn't keep my eyes off you. But I never approached you until Alexis excused herself and left me to man the bar by myself, because I always thought-"

"What?" I wonder aloud. My breath already catches in my throat, and my eyes are glued to his again while waiting for his answer. A little bead of sweat collects on his brow and it's the only indicator I see that he's even half as nervous as I am right now. Because throughout, he still has his hand on mine, and he's still caressing me. Perhaps he needs that comfort as much as I do.

"I was certain I'd put you off by looking over at you all the time. That you'd run as soon as I opened my mouth."

"Evidently, I did run. But that wasn't the reason," I explain, still barely able to get the words out at a reasonable volume. It's a miracle he hears me at all, nevermind understanding every word.

"Why, then?" he urges.

"Because it's what I do. Because the intensity of what happened overwhelmed me. Similarly, I thought there was no way you'd ever be interested in someone like me." I blurt it out before even considering whether it's a good idea to tell him this. But he did. He showed his insecurities first. It made me feel safe enough to share myself.

"Someone like you?" he asks, his eyes holding mine gently.

"You know, boring, bookish, plain…"

A smile breaks through his formerly concerned expression. "You are none of those things. Except bookish, perhaps, but I consider that a plus."

"Well, I guess we both have some issues in how we perceive ourselves," I say.

He's still smiling, and I find that, actually, so am I. Again.

"I want to say something, but I worry it's out of turn." He holds my hand more firmly now, which feels nice. Grounded. Even his hands are handsome. Does that even make sense? Strong, comforting… manly.

"Just tell me," I press.

He takes a deep breath and holds my gaze again. "I want to make it clear that I'm not trying to rush or pressure you, but… I can't stop thinking about how it felt to kiss you."

Oh hell. How am I supposed to convince myself or him that I'm 'not that type of girl,' when he seems so intent on luring her out at every turn? I could eat this man up. I could…

I don't, of course. I take a long, ragged breath to try and ignore what his entire being does to my hormones.

"That's been…" I exhale sharply before finishing my thought.

"Yes?" he asks.

"That kiss is the highlight of my life, honestly."

CHAPTER TEN

*** Nathan ***

Those words, coming from her perfect lips, will be etched in my memory forever. And everything that follows now is just the icing on the cake.

We finish our food quickly, barely talking anymore. Although the restaurant has quite a tempting array of desserts to offer, we both decline, eager to get somewhere more private. I pay the bill in a rush to join her outside, arm in arm, to take a walk through the quiet streets.

"I don't want you to think I expect anything," I tell her.

She squeezes my arm and rests her head on my shoulder. "Thank you."

Having her head there feels like the most natural thing in the world, as though she's always belonged by my side. And yet, the rush of anticipation in my stomach is so strong, because this *is* new. This is uncharted territory in many ways, for both of us.

Despite that, the crisp night air helps me feel grounded enough to savor every step on our way.

You're welcome, I think, but I dare not say a word for fear of breaking this spell.

We walk a few more minutes in comfortable silence. It's charged. I feel her thoughts humming, even if she keeps them locked away. I want to ask what's going through her mind, but a part of me is content to wait until she's ready.

When we reach a historic brick building adjoining a small park a few streets over from the High Street, she slows. I stop with her, turning to face her under the dim glow of the streetlight.

"This is me," she says softly, almost apologetically, like she wishes it weren't.

I don't want to leave. God, I don't want this night to end. But I don't want to push, either. I vowed that I wouldn't. "I had an incredible time, Jane. I'd love to do this again soon."

She lifts her eyes, meeting mine. "Me, too." The words are quiet, but sincere.

For a long, suspended moment, neither of us moves. I'm caught between the pull of her lips and the fear of moving too fast, of scaring her away.

Despite her admission that our kiss meant as much to her as it did to me, and the fact that my body continues to react viscerally to her presence, I refuse to force the issue or make a move yet. I just stand here, captivated by her gaze, waiting for her permission.

It's subtle, but she stirs. A twitch in her shoulder, a tremble in her hand as it reaches for me.

"I really like you, Nathan," she tells me, while she holds my hand.

Those words send a shiver down my spine. I guess I hadn't realized how badly I needed to hear them. Being chosen by the one you want.

"I really like you, and I want nothing more than to invite you in." She exhales sharply, and glances down at my lips.

That's what I want, too, but you're not ready, I mentally complete her sentence. *Kiss me. Please.*

"Do you?" she asks, eyes wide, the whites of them catching in the light from the streetlamp overhead. "Do you want to come in?"

That's even better. "I'd love to."

"Just to talk some more. In private…" she adds, eyebrows pulled together as if she expects rejection or disappointment.

"I could talk to you all night," I respond. "Or just keep holding your hand. Your pick."

Relieved, she smiles, and I'm on top of the world.

This girl is an enigma, able to surprise me at any turn. Did I want to do more than talk? Of course; none of my earlier sordid desires have faded much, but also… Just the prospect of spending a few more minutes in her presence makes me feel like I've already won. I've seen how skittish she can be. How hard it is for her to put herself out there and open up to me. For her to allow me into her home-her sanctuary-that means something. For whatever reason, she trusts me. I'll be damned if I ever break that trust. No matter what I desire from her physically.

"Okay, but don't mind the mess, okay?" she says while turning to unlock the ornate wooden front door.

"Couldn't be worse than my place," I mumble.

She shoots a grateful smile my way while pushing the door open and leading the way inside.

I follow on autopilot, taking it all in. As we head inside the tiled lobby and up the winding staircase to what looks to be an attic apartment, I feel like I'm climbing into a secret hideaway. Even from outside her front door, the scent of old books fills my nostrils. It's lovely, mysterious and also comforting. Much like Jane herself.

The inside of her cramped living space makes me smile. It's not a mess per se, but it's full. Floor to ceiling shelves with books, magazines, notebooks, and newspapers covering most of the space. Although it's a lot, it's also organized. Books lined up in color-coded blocks where she's clearly grouped series or imprints together. Magazines and newspapers have their own little racks and stacks. In the middle, there's a generous red velvet sofa covered with an old fashioned crochet throw draped across the armrest with colorful embroidered cushions grouped in either corner.

It's like she sought out to create the perfect reading nook, except that's her entire living room.

"Make yourself comfortable. I'll just get us something to drink," she says while rushing off into the adjoining kitchen.

"I'm quite okay, thanks," I call after her.

Still, she returns carrying two mismatched vintage wine glasses and a bottle of something I can't quite identify. "I'm sorry, I'm not much of a drinker, so I don't think this is going to be very good. It was a gift."

She puts the whole lot down on the cozy wooden coffee table that fills the space between the sofa and the wall unit that houses a modestly-sized TV and yet more books. Immediately after, she snatches up what looks like a scrapbook, closing it and hugging it tightly against her chest.

"I'm quite happy to just talk, please relax," I tell her, gesturing at her to sit with me.

Her eyes still dart around the room, seeking out and settling on anything she must perceive as 'messy' or out of place.

"I love your home. It's very warm and inviting," I tell her. *And charming like you.*

"I imagine yours is all leather and chrome furniture

and classy vintage prints on the walls," she blurts out.

This makes me laugh. I do actually have a collection of vintage beer advertisements hanging on my wall. And a well-worn brown leather armchair that wouldn't look out of place in an old fashioned gentleman's club, or indeed, the White Hart. Am I so predictable?

"I like yours better," I say. In fact, I'd happily stay here forever.

She smiles and puts the journal down on one of the shelves before taking a seat.

"I've never had a guy in here," she comments.

"It's an honor to be the first," I reply.

Her head turns in my direction and she just stares. There's a faint tremble in her bottom lip. When she speaks again, it's obvious she chooses her words carefully. "What I meant when I said dating, and flirting, and all of that wasn't me… I meant it quite literally. You're the first there, too."

My heart, as well as the rest of my body reacts powerfully to her confession. It's a mixture of relief, hope, and sheer need to reach over and hold her. But I resist. Because I see that she's nervous. Of judgement, and maybe of the entire situation we find ourselves in.

She can't be much younger than me. Mid to late twenties, maybe. Did she really never want to, until me, now? That's ludicrous.

I can relate, though. Although I've been in relationships before, even been burned before, I still feel there's something different about her. About how she makes me feel. As such, it's almost new territory for me, too.

"That's an honor, too," I tell her, my voice lower and raspier than I planned for it to be.

She blows out a sigh of relief and settles down beside me, her head ending up on my shoulder again. I'm floating, my mind spinning out of control. I feel the warmth of her body through the fabric of her sweater dress, the weight of her trust pressed up against me.

For a moment, I just sit there-utterly still-so I don't break it.

I glance at her profile, the way a stray strand of blonde hair has fallen loose from her updo, curling against her cheek. She's so close that I could reach out and brush it back. My fingers twitch at the thought, but I force them to stay put.

"Jane?" I murmur, not because I have anything to say, but because I want to hear her name leave my lips.

"Mmm?" she answers, voice muffled against my shoulder.

"I just want to be completely clear… you don't have to prove anything to me. Not tonight. Not ever. I'll never pressure you." *We can go exactly as far and as slow as you want,* I add in thought.

She lifts her head slightly to look at me, eyes wide and searching, like she's trying to decide whether she believes me.

"You're not… disappointed?"

"Disappointed?" I repeat, half a laugh escaping me. "I'm sitting here with the most beautiful woman I've ever met, in her secret little world of books, feeling her heart beat against my arm. How could I possibly be disappointed?"

Her breath catches-one small, sharp inhale-and then she laughs quietly. It's nervous at first, then softens into something almost shy. "You're very… unexpected," she says.

"Good unexpected, I hope."

"Yeah," she whispers. "Perfect."

Her eyes drop to my mouth for a fraction of a second before darting away again, and that flicker of hesitation-want tangled with fear-does something to me. I feel my pulse thrumming in my ears, but I hold still. I don't move until she does.

And then, so carefully I almost don't register it, she shifts closer, coaxing my arm up and around her shoulders, my hand draping down her side. Her other hand reaches up to it, tentative but deliberate. I spread my fingers, letting hers slide into them. She exhales again, the kind of breath you take when you're finally safe.

Although I'm tense and indeed as aroused as ever, in her presence, a deep sense of calm also comes over me. This is when it strikes me just how different she is. How different we are together. This isn't a mere first date, it's so much more.

We sit there, my arm around her and hands entwined, surrounded by the scent of old paper and the soft ticking of a clock somewhere behind us, whiling the minutes away. Just being in each other's presence, breathing in each other's scent, while occasionally talking a little more.

Nothing happens. And yet-I'm done for.

CHAPTER ELEVEN

*** Jane ***

I can't stop smiling. It's ridiculous. Utterly, hopelessly ridiculous.

I've reorganized the same stack of books three times now, and I still can't remember where the last one is supposed to go. It's as if all the Dewey Decimal numbers have blurred into a single glowing thought: *Nathan.*

Nathan, walking me home.

Nathan, in my living room.

Nathan, saying things that took my breath away.

Nathan, who didn't kiss me again last night, even though every fiber of my being wanted him to.

That part plays on repeat in my head. The restraint. The quiet understanding. The way his thumb brushed the back of my hand, like he was memorizing it. Who *does* that? Who just… holds your hand like it's the most natural, intimate thing in the world? When I know how he reacted to me the first night; how turned on he was. How I led him on and then pulled the plug, and rather than complain about it or show any hint of impatience, he just… He just seemed happy to see me again. And yes, I could see his eyes burning with desire throughout dinner, but he made good on his word and didn't rush me in any way. He must be a saint.

I glance down at my fingers now, half expecting to still feel the imprint of his. It's embarrassing how easily I drift off into the memory. My cheeks are still sore this morning from smiling so much.

This must be what people mean when they say 'on cloud nine.' I didn't think it was a real thing-just a saying in books. But here I am, floating somewhere above the ground, completely useless as a librarian and completely smitten with a man I still hardly know.

Is this love?

No, it can't be. That would be insane.

But maybe… the start of it?

"Jane."

The sound of my name jolts me back to earth. I look up and see Vicky standing at the end of the aisle, arms folded, wearing her trademark *I know something's up* expression.

"Morning," I say, far too brightly.

"Morning," she echoes in a tone that's half suspicion, half amusement. "You're… very different today."

I blink innocently. "Am I?"

She arches her brow. "You *whistled* while you were shelving."

I freeze. "No, I didn't."

"You did," she says firmly. "And you were humming something that sounded suspiciously like a love song. So either you've discovered a new genre of library cataloguing joy, or…" She pauses, eyes narrowing. "Is it about that guy, Nathan?"

My heart skips at the mention of his name. "That's absurd."

"Is it?" she says. "Because you've been walking around like someone sprinkled fairy dust on your morning tea. And unless you finally found that missing copy of Wuthering Heights, I'm calling it-you're being very suspicious."

I open my mouth, but nothing comes out. Words, lies, excuses-they all turn to mush in my brain. I look down at the book in my hand, desperate for an escape.

"It's just… a beautiful day today," I say weakly.

"Uh-huh." She leans against the shelf. "You, my dear, have *Good Day Syndrome* . Symptoms include dreamy smiles, distracted sighs, and spontaneous whistling. Usually caused by kissing someone you shouldn't."

"Nathan and I didn't kiss!" I blurt out, then immediately curse myself, because that only makes her raise her eyebrows higher.

"So it *is* about him! Sweetie, I told you already that he's bad news. And this right here-" She gestures me up and down as if to illustrate some genius point. "This is confirmation. It's not healthy."

I groan, pressing the heel of my hand to my forehead. "Vicky, please."

"Oh, I see. We think we know better than paranoid old Vicky." She gestures dramatically.

"That's not fair," I mutter under my breath.

"Fine, fine," she says, holding up her hands in surrender-her expression softer than before. "Be happy. Follow your heart. I'll still be here for you when you figure out the truth."

The truth is, I think I might just be in love, or something like it. With Nathan. Who she thinks is a great big walking red flag. But how do I explain to her that he isn't without sharing details of last night, which I don't feel like sharing? I don't have the romantic experience she has, but I'm not naive and stupid, am I? Do I not have valid instincts? So far all of mine tell me that he's perfect, and I'm the one who's lacking.

And yes, I get how suspicious that would seem to a third party like her. Our lives have followed a very different course so far. And although we've shared a lot, there are certain topics we've never covered. Like my history with men, or lack thereof. And whatever happened to her that made her this paranoid. Unless it's all the dark romance she's been reading, which she tends to refer to as 'nice from far, but far from nice.'

So I just smile faintly and say, "Thank you Vicky. Let's not let anything-or anyone-come between our friendship."

She nods and wanders off again, leaving me to my stack of biographies and my thoughts. It takes me a minute to unwind from our conversation. And soon, I catch myself quietly humming again.

*** Nathan ***

The evening drags on like molasses. Not because there aren't customers-far from it-but because I can't concentrate. I'm serving pints, cleaning glasses and wiping the counter largely on autopilot. Eventually I'm half-listening to some guy debate craft beer as though he's holding a TED Talk, all while my mind keeps drifting back to Jane.

Her laugh. That small, quick smile she gives when she breaks eye contact. Her eyes widen whenever she looks at me. The way she rested her head on my shoulder last night, as if it always belonged there. My chest tightens at the memory. I spill a little lager on the bar and curse under my breath, drawing a curious glance from Alexis.

"Feeling okay there, Nathan?" she asks, her eyebrow raised in suspicion. "You've got a bit of a… look going on. Something on your mind?"

I straighten up and force a shrug. "All good, just didn't sleep particularly much," I say.

"Uh-huh." She leans on the counter, elbows resting on the polished wood. "And why has our friendly neighborhood bartender been missing out on his much needed beauty sleep? Anything I need to know about? It's not that same girl again, is it? Not that it's any of my business."

I groan, trying not to smile while continuing to clean. "Indeed, Alexis. Not your business."

"Only trying to make sure we're not going to have any more incidents," she replies with mock solemnity.

I tilt my head, then nod. "Yeah, no, no more incidents. We managed to clear the air between us, Jane and I."

Her eyes soften, and she claps me lightly on the shoulder while grabbing a couple of ciders out of the fridge between us. "Good. Well, then. Glad it all worked out, Nathan. Seriously."

"Thanks," I mutter, feeling a surge of warmth in my chest.

***

The night outside is crisp and clear when my shift finally ends. The streets are quieter now, the old fashioned lanterns gracing the facade of the historic pub fading in the distance behind me. I should head straight home, but my feet have other plans.

Somehow, they carry me past Jane's street. Not a detour, not really… just a small bend in the route that makes sense to my restless legs.

There it is-her building, cozy yet historic, the little touches in the darkened windows hinting at the very special person living inside. I stop for a moment, letting myself just look at it. Not watching. Just… noticing. Feeling a pull I can't explain.

I reach into my coat pocket to retrieve a tiny trinket I purchased for no reason at all earlier today-until its purpose became very clear indeed. A miniature journal, its gilded edges catching the dim streetlight, fashioned into a keyring. Pretty, delicate, something she might like. Something that, in my mind, says: *I remember you. I'm thinking of you. You're special to me.*

I slip it into her letterbox quietly, a small thrill running through me. Not a grand gesture, not a declaration-but a marker. A way to say, *I'm here. I'm thinking of you. And I'm not going anywhere.*

As I walk away, heart still hammering, I feel like a teenager again. Smitten. Head over heels. And terrified. Terrified of getting too close, only for her to figure me out. Terrified of what happens once she realizes I'm not nearly as interesting as she seems to think right now-but unable to stop myself from wanting her anyway.

It's intoxicating. And I wouldn't trade it for anything.

CHAPTER TWELVE

*** Jane ***

The little thing is exquisite.

A miniature journal with gilt-edged pages, no bigger than a matchbox, bound in soft, navy-blue leather, fashioned into a keyring. When I found it in my letterbox this morning, I didn't need to think twice to know who it was from.

Nathan. Of course it was Nathan.

There was no note attached-just the tiny book itself, gleaming quietly in my palm. But somehow, that made it even more meaningful. Subtle. Thoughtful. Like something out of a slow burn regency romance.

Now, hours later, it sits on my desk at the library, next to my mug of lukewarm tea. Every time I glance at it, I smile. Every time I pick it up, a little flutter kicks up in my stomach.

I don't even realize I'm staring at it again until I hear Vicky's voice behind me.

"Oh my God," she says. "You've got that look again."

I drop the keyring onto the desk and grab my mug to deflect. "What look?"

"The love-struck one." She circles the desk like a hawk, eyes narrowing at the object in question. "What have you got there?"

"Nothing," I say too quickly, brushing it aside with my hand.

"Nothing," she repeats, plucking it off the desk before I can stop her. "Oh, wow, it's… precious actually. And completely not something one would buy for oneself." Her gaze snaps up to mine. "Tell me it's not him."

I swallow. "Vicky-"

"Oh, Jane," she groans, pressing her fingers to her temples. "You can't be serious. You said you weren't seeing him again!"

"I *never* said that," I protest weakly. "And I haven't seen him again." Not last night, anyway.

She gives me a sharp look. "I'm telling you, he's bad news."

I sigh, trying to maintain some sort of calmness, but I can't resist the urge to defend myself. Or him. Whatever. "He's been really lovely, Vic. Thoughtful. We've been messaging a little, and… it's nice. He's not what you think."

"Messaging how?" she presses. "Like *nice-guy* nice? Or love-bombing before turning psycho nice?"

"Vicky," I say, exasperated. "Surely those aren't the

only two options. What if he's a genuinely kind person? Nathan isn't Joe from *You!*"

Her cheeks turn a shade darker, and I wonder if I've hit a raw nerve. Is that what it is? Is she speaking from experience, not Netflix?

She crosses her arms. "I just don't want you getting hurt. Little gifts, how obsessed you seem with him already-those are *red flags*, Jane. You're head over heels, but you've seen him in person, what, twice or thrice?"

"If only you knew," I mumble under my breath. I spent so many nights at the White Hart this past month watching him, I managed to fill pages of my journal with ramblings about the man formerly known as BB before ever speaking one word to him.

I take the keyring back from her, gripping it tightly in my hand while watching her walk away again. Vicky's warnings water the seed of doubt she'd planted earlier. She's right about one thing: I barely know Nathan. I only learned his last name from the library card application form I snuck a peek at earlier, and still have no clue what his family is like, or whether he prefers cats or dogs. I don't even know how he takes his coffee in the morning or if he drinks tea instead.

All I know is that he seems gentle, warm, and makes me feel seen in a way I didn't think possible. He's the first. My first love, no matter how wild that seems after an ill-advised kiss and a subsequent dinner date.

Am I being naive? Is this what falling in love is supposed to feel like-this constant tug between excitement and fear? Of doing something wrong, or perhaps just of everything blowing up in my face… It's a rollercoaster for sure. Terrifying yet addictive.

When my phone buzzes moments later, I still can't help myself. A surge of excitement hits me straight in the chest when I see it's Nathan. Again.

Hope your day is going okay. Just wanted to let you know I might've walked past your street on my way home from work last night. My feet seemed to just carry me there. I hope you don't mind.

My heart melts. He hopes I don't mind? God, that's adorable, after I've essentially stalked him for weeks.

I type back before I can stop myself.

If you're trying to play it cool, you're failing.

He sends a laughing emoji, followed by: *Busted. I can't wait to see you again, by the way. How about I cook for you tonight? My place. Nothing fancy-just dinner and a chance to get to know each other some more without interruptions.*

I hesitate, staring at the screen. Dinner at his place. That's so… intimate.

An annoying voice chirps up in the back of my head. *He's expecting something! Red flag!*

I try to shake it off, because Nathan has given me

no reason to think like that. He told me on Monday night that he'd never pressure me. That was genuine, wasn't it? That was real.

Finally, I reply: *That sounds wonderful. What time?*

He replies quickly. He suggests we meet at seven p.m., sending me his address and a location pin followed by a heart. Just one. Simple, small. It sends my pulse soaring all over again.

Maybe Vicky's right. Maybe I *am* being naive. But it feels so good to believe in him, in us. Soft, hopeful, and impossibly alive. I don't want to let it go just yet. This fragile stage of yearning and not knowing, it's my favorite of any romance novel. It makes sense that I'd be hooked in real life too. Three hours until the end of my workday. Another hour to get ready and head to Nathan's place which is a comfortable walk from my flat. It seems impossibly distant, yet also much too soon.

*** Nathan ***

The moment I put my phone down, I realize what I've done and my earlier smile at Jane's acceptance fades.

Dinner at *my place*. Tonight.

Bloody hell.

Why did I suggest that? Why not coffee, or a walk, or something less… loaded? She said yes so quickly that I barely had time to think, but now-standing in the middle of my tiny kitchen, staring at an open cupboard and realizing I own exactly one clean wine glass-I'm very much panicking.

It's not like I meant for it to sound like a seduction. I just wanted more time with her. To talk. To see her without the background noise of the pub or the awkward presence of wait staff at a restaurant. Just her and me, gazing into each other's eyes in peace.

And honestly, it's my only night off this week. If I didn't ask to see her tonight, I wouldn't have had another chance until next Monday.

Still. Dinner at home. What the hell was I thinking?

I rummage through the cupboards again, muttering to myself. "Right. Food. Keep it simple. Stick to what you know."

Pasta. Always reliable. And I've still got a jar of Genovese pesto straight from Italy, plus a few potatoes that haven't sprouted or turned to mush yet. Pasta alla ligure, with basil, potatoes, and green beans. Just like I'd seen on that new cooking show recently. It's humble, easy, forgiving and yet different enough to look impressive. At least, that's what the chef on TV said about it.

I should tidy up first. I should… Looking around, I feel overwhelmed all over again. I'm normally quite neat and tidy, despite what I told her to reassure her when she apologized about the mess at her place, but… The dishes. I should do the dishes. And dust the furniture. And definitely sweep up whatever mess I end up making while cooking.

Breathing deeply a few times, I decide to get started. I have time. Still, my hands tremble a little while I start on the pile of plates and cups and bowls I've neglected for two days. That's how obsessed I've been with her. It's a miracle I managed to get up, brush my teeth, shower, and dress myself every day.

As expected-or feared-the afternoon passes all too quickly.

I chop, boil, taste, fuss, and try to clean as I go. The kitchen smells good-warm, garlicky, promising-but then I get distracted watching the clock and overcook the pasta by a minute or two. Maybe three. The potatoes are too soft now too, collapsing slightly when I toss everything together. Brilliant. Not so easy and forgiving after all, then.

I should've just ordered a pizza.

Still, I try to plate it nicely before popping it in the oven to keep it warm, and set my tiny kitchen-table-for-two. A bottle of extra virgin olive oil, some grated parmesan in a bowl, pretending I know what I'm doing. I even light a candle, immediately feeling like an idiot for doing so, and blow it out again. Too much. She's not even here yet.

Now all that's left is to wait.

And pace.

And check the mirror by the door at least six times, wondering if I should've trimmed my beard or worn a different shirt.

It's ridiculous how much I want this to go well. How I've spent half the day imagining the look on her face when she walks in. Not because I'm hoping for anything beyond dinner-but because I want her to feel safe. Comfortable. Welcome.

I need her to know she can trust me.

When the doorbell finally rings, I nearly trip over my own feet getting there.

There she is, wrapped in that same red coat she always wears, hair windblown, cheeks rosy from the cold, blinking against the sharp wind. She's holding a six-pack of craft beer, smiling up at me in that disarming fashion of hers.

"Hey," she speaks softly. "I thought this might be more to your taste than the obligatory bottle of wine."

It's perfect. Absolutely perfect.

"Thank you, though it wasn't necessary. Come on in," I say quickly, taking the beers to free up her hands. Her fingers brush mine and for a second, I forget every word I've ever known.

She steps inside, shaking off the chill and rubbing her hands together, and I'm instantly aware of how the place smells intrusively of garlic. Oh god, I'm sure I must absolutely reek of the stuff.

"You're freezing," I blurt out. "Let me get you a blanket. Or tea. Or-"

"Nathan." She laughs, interrupting me with a mere look. "It's okay. I'm fine. The wind was a bit chilly, but it's perfectly warm here."

That voice, that smile-it's enough to melt me.

Suddenly all the fretting about the pasta, the wine glass, the candle, all of it just… fades.

She's here. And that's magical in itself.

"Right," I say, rubbing the back of my neck awkwardly. "Dinner's ready. The pasta might be slightly overcooked, but I hope it still tastes okay."

She laughs again while taking off her coat before following me through the hallway. "Smells perfectly lovely to me. And anyway, I'm starving. Thank you so much for doing this, because I'm not much of a cook."

For the first time all afternoon and evening, I take a breath. And I stop worrying. I just *feel.* Grateful that she's here. That I got to cook this meal for her. That I get to listen to her tell me about her day at the library. About how excited she got at a delivery of new books. And how sometimes she sneaks away to read if it's a particularly quiet day, but lately she's just been reading my texts.

In turn, I tell her about my work. That I'd considered becoming a chef once upon a time, but settled on bartending, because as a night owl, the timings suit me better. By the time we finish our slightly stodgy lukewarm dinner, I offer her ice cream for dessert and she declines. I half expect her to tell me she has an early start tomorrow, and must head home, but instead she offers to help with the dishes.

"No way. Nope. I'm not having you do chores the first time you're at my place," I say.

She suppresses a smile. "But you did all the cooking!"

I continue shaking my head. "My place, my chores. And anyway, this all needs to soak first."

"At least let me do that, then," she urges.

I fold my arms and block the way towards the sink. "Nope. Please make yourself comfortable in the living area, and I'll join you in a second."

She reluctantly hands me the plates and retreats towards the large leather couch. And I do everything in my power to dump all the dirty plates in the sink as quickly as possible so I can spend the rest of the evening with her. Obsessed. As I said.

CHAPTER THIRTEEN

*** Jane ***

Nathan's place is how I thought it would be. Modern, masculine, somewhat minimalist, but not sterile. It's open plan and surprisingly airy, considering it's essentially a studio with an attached kitchen. Spotting the 1950s beer advertisement posters on the wall above the black leather sofa make me chuckle a bit. I totally called it.

And the food tastes heavenly, despite his warnings. The looks he shoots my way throughout dinner warm me up from the inside out. As does the pasta. Who would have thought that the combination of pesto, potatoes, and green beans could be this comforting?

It's because he cooked it, I tell myself. It's all him.

When he sheepishly admits he forgot to pick up drinks for our dinner date, we instead decide to sample the six-pack I brought. Although for me, water would have been just fine.

After dinner, we settle on the large leather couch and talk for hours-sharing childhood anecdotes, favorite songs, the strange things we've both googled at two a.m. It's easy. So easy that I forget what time it is, or that I'm supposed to be a sensible adult who usually goes to bed by twelve.

One thing leads to another and somehow, I end up staying.

It's nothing like I'd imagined that first night together would be. No fireworks, no urgency. Just us, curled up on his sofa, the glow of a modern reading lamp painting everything in soft gold. His arm around me feels safe, grounding, and yet my heart continues to race as if it hasn't quite caught up to how peaceful the moment is.

His presence does that to me now, from the moment I finally confessed my truth to him on Monday. Those broad shoulders that could carry the world. Strong beautiful hands that treat me so gently, it brings tears to my eyes. I'd be lying to myself if I didn't acknowledge how utterly sexy he is. Precisely because he is a gentle giant. Solid, dependable, but full of hidden passion, if our kiss that first night is anything to go by. He's got a wild side to him, which he keeps locked away for my benefit. Because he knows I'm not ready. But as soon as I will be… Oh boy.

We must have talked for hours. His voice grows slower, lower, until at some point, we just… drift into silence. I fall asleep to the sound of his heartbeat, the faint hum of the fridge, the warmth of a woolen throw tucked around my shoulders and the steadiness of his breaths caressing my hair.

When I wake up, my arm clinging possessively to his waist, sunlight streams through the blinds already. My mouth is dry, my head foggy-and… I jerk up in a panic.

"Oh crap," I whisper, fumbling for my bag. "My alarm-Nathan, what time is it?"

He startles awake next to me. His hair and beard are adorably mussed when he looks up and checks his watch. "Almost nine."

"*Nine?* I'm supposed to be at work, like, right now!"

I scramble onto my feet, putting my boots back on, all while trying to smooth my hair into something vaguely professional, before settling on a messy bun because all other options are hopeless. Oh my god, do I need a shower? What about my breath?

Nathan jumps into action as well, rushing into the kitchen where he boils the kettle and quickly mixes together a few ingredients into a cup.

"I'm so sorry," he says, pressing a steaming mug of milky instant coffee into my hands. "This is totally my fault. You can blame me."

"I've never been late in the entire time I've worked there." My heart races, but when our eyes meet and I see the anguish in his, I pause and take a breath. And a sip of coffee, which helps to steady my anxiety. And another. "I suppose I've earned some goodwill over the years, even if I am tardy today. Thanks for the coffee."

His panicked expression softens into a crooked smile. "I didn't pause to ask how you take it."

"It's perfect. Everything about last night was perfect too, by the way." Dear lord, save me from myself.

"You're welcome. Literally any time." His voice has an edge to it. An emotion I can't quite identify, only that it's a good one.

"Watch out, or I might just take you up on that. But I've really got to go now." I hand him the half-empty mug back.

"If not, I'll leave little bribes in your letterbox to win you over." He knows just what to say to melt my heart.

As I reach for the door, he helps me into my coat like an old-fashioned gentleman. My feet suddenly grow heavier. It's ridiculous how much I don't want to leave.

"See you later, Nathan," I say, giving him a little hug without thinking. "Love you."

The words tumble out before I can stop them. And then the silence hits, and my heart all but stops beating.

Nathan's eyes widen, surprise flickering across his face-but then, before I find the words to backpedal or break the tension, he steps closer.

"Hey," he says softly. "You know what? I love you, too."

I can't breathe. I can't think. He cups my face and kisses me-slow, deep, and certain. Our second kiss is as intense as the first, but also completely different. Because this time, it doesn't follow performative flirtations or pure base instinct. This right here is it. The real deal. This isn't the end goal. It's the beginning of something beautiful.

When we finally pull apart, I'm dizzy. Maybe from how his kiss took my breath away, maybe from the fact that I'm already panicking about being late for work. Or maybe, because I'm on top of the entire world because he feels the same.

"Go," he murmurs, brushing a strand of hair from my cheek. "Before you get into trouble."

I rush out the door with a stupid grin on my face, my heart light and yet overflowing with hope and promise.

By the time I reach the library, cheeks flushed and hair even messier than it already was, I'm past caring about appearances. If I have to kick these heels off and work the whole day in my tights to avoid blisters, that's cool too.

Because for once, everything in my life feels exactly right. The last piece I was missing finally fell into place.

I'm in love. And it feels like the sun's come out to shine just for me.

*** Nathan ***

I can't stop replaying it in my head.

Love you.

Two little words that have detonated in my chest like fireworks, and I'm still dazed in the aftermath.

I must have stood in my doorway for a full five minutes after she left, just staring at the empty space she'd occupied, grinning like an idiot. Her coffee mug still sits on the counter, a little droplet stuck on the rim where her lips touched. I should probably wash it. But I can't bring myself to-not yet. It feels like proof. Like evidence that this morning actually happened.

She loves me. How? And why? But then, why not? Because I do, too.

God, I can't even remember the last time I felt this light. I'm still half-buzzed from it, half-terrified it'll fade if I move too quickly.

I try to read a little, but my concentration's shot to hell. I keep checking my phone, willing it to light up. By eleven, I give in and send her a message first.

I can't stop thinking about you. Fancy lunch at your regular spot, Coffee to the Rescue? I have a few hours before my shift starts.

Jane: Would love to! My break starts at 12:30.

Perfect.

By the time I leave my flat, I'm practically whistling. The world looks different today. The sky's brighter, the air fresher, the city somehow friendlier. Even the bus driver who had to stop for me at the zebra crossing smiles when I give him a little thank-you wave.

When I step into Alice's café, the scent of coffee and cinnamon rolls hits me like a warm hug. Alice herself is behind the counter, wiping her hands on a pale pink tea towel.

"Wow, Nathan, look at you," she says, one eyebrow cocked. "You look so… Happy! It's quite the contrast to the last time you came in."

I chuckle. "I suppose."

"Uh-huh." She crosses her arms, grinning. "Am I to assume that you did indeed take my advice and went to the library that day? And it all worked out?"

Normally I'd deflect, change the subject, but not today. Today, I grin at her like the Cheshire cat. "Something like that."

Alice laughs and shakes her head. "Brilliant. I'm taking full credit, just so you know. A number of folks have found love right here in this fine establishment. Something about the vibes of this place. I should have Amber include it in our marketing."

"Fair. You were right and I do owe you," I say, slipping a note into the tip jar.

"Hey now, at least order something first," Alice urges with a smile. "And I'm happy to take payment in thank-yous and flattery."

"Now, that I can do. I'll have one of your excellent double espressos, and another of those delicious caramel brownies, please. And whatever Jane wants when she gets here, of course. Thanks, Alice!" I shoot one last smile Alice's way before making my way over to that same table at the far end of the café. Just because I'm okay with Alice knowing about Jane and me doesn't mean I want her to listen in on our conversations, too.

Soon after I take my seat, Alice places my order in front of me with a smile. I can't bring myself to touch it, though. Not the coffee and not the brownie either. Instead, I check my watch every few seconds like a man possessed.

Twelve twenty-seven.

Twelve twenty-eight.

Twelve twenty-nine.

Any second now, Jane'll walk through that door-and everything will feel right again.

CHAPTER FOURTEEN

*** Jane ***

I can't stop smiling. It's ridiculous. Every time I think about this morning-his sleepy grin and tousled hair, the warmth of his hand on my back, the way he said*I love you, too* without hesitation and that earth shattering kiss after-my insides flutter all over again.

I've replayed it a hundred times already. It was messy, unplanned, too soon, and perfect.

As such, I can't concentrate on the paperwork I'm supposed to finish. Instead, I re-read our exchange from earlier while watching the time creep ever closer to twelve-thirty.

I can't stop thinking about you. Fancy lunch at your regular spot, Coffee to the Rescue? I have a few hours before my shift starts.

My grin widens. My regular spot, so perceptive of him. The words make my chest bloom with something soft and sweet. The little heart he sent after my response means even more to me after everything that's happened this morning. But my bliss is interrupted by a piercing cough right behind me.

I spin around to find Vicky leaning against the end of the desk, arms crossed, and her expression sharp enough to slice through glass.

"How long have you been standing there?" I ask.

"Long enough," she says. "So. He figured out where you work, knows where you live... and he knows about our regular lunch spot. Did you tell him about all that, or did he conveniently guess that too?" Her eyes flick to my phone, still glowing on the counter. "And judging by what you're wearing, I guess you went on a date and then never made it home last night."

Heat rushes to my cheeks. Never made it home... So what? She's stayed the night with men before, and probably done a whole lot more than I did with Nathan.

"It's not what you think," I stammer.

"Oh, really? Enlighten me."

I fold my arms, trying not to sound defensive but failing miserably. "He cooked me dinner from scratch-pasta with pesto and potatoes-it was lovely. And then we stayed up and talked until we fell asleep on the couch. He's kind, and thoughtful, and..."

"And?" Vicky arches a brow.

"And we have actual *feelings* for each other, okay?" I say.

Vicky exhales sharply, shaking her head as if I've confessed to investing my life's savings into a pyramid scheme. "Jane, this is way too intense. You barely know the man."

"I know him a lot better after talking for hours last

night, whereas you don't know him at all," I counter.

"Oh yeah? You've been on what-two dates? He's probably just telling you what you want to hear."

"Nathan isn't like that," I insist, my voice trembling. "He's genuine." Although… I don't recall actually telling him that Coffee to the Rescue is my regular lunch spot… I frown. Maybe he guessed it somehow.

"Genuine?" she snaps. "This is textbook grooming, Jane. Gifts, flattery, intensity, along with this whole good-guy routine he seems to have down pat-he's love bombing you, making you feel special so you'll let your guard down and spread your legs. It's not love, it's manipulation."

My stomach twists. I can hear the echo of my mother's voice in hers: *Men only want one thing. Don't be easy!*

I swallow, forcing the words out before I can stop myself. "It's not like that! We *really* love each other, Vicky. It's like in all the best books. Love at first sight."

Her jaw drops. "You-what? Are you hearing yourself right now?"

"We do. He told me this morning."

Vicky stares at me like I've just announced I'm joining a cult. "Jane, you can't be serious. He's definitely love bombing you. Romance novels aren't reality. Nobody falls in love at first sight or after a couple of dates. He's pushing fast so you'll ignore the red flags."

But, I did! I fell in love at first sight. Does my experience not matter?

"There are no red flags!" I protest, but the sound of my own voice wobbles. "We didn't even-there was nothing physical, except a kiss. That's it. It's been completely wholesome and innocent."

"Don't you see?" she says, her pitch rising with frantic conviction. "He's trying to get you comfortable so he *can* get in your pants. You're playing hard to get, and he's the type who likes a challenge. I observed him at the pub that night. He's smooth, that one. Confident. Knows how to get what he wants. Once he gets it from you, he'll be gone before you can blink."

The words hit something raw and familiar inside me-the same old fear, the shame, the desperate need not to be *that kind of girl.* The one my mother accused me of being way back when. After the unthinkable happened to me. My throat closes up, and suddenly everything Vicky says blurs into one relentless buzz I can't seem to escape.

"He's not. He won't," I whisper, but it's weak now. I don't sound convinced, even to myself. And more than that, I don't have the energy to counter her anymore. Her onslaught of relentless complaints has overwhelmed me and rendered me defenseless. I want to run; hide from this feeling, but my legs don't carry me anymore. And anyway, you can't outrun the voices in your own head. I've learned that the hard way.

Vicky softens slightly, mistaking my silence for surrender. "You don't have to face him alone, okay? You've got me. I'm not letting you meet him for coffee all by yourself."

"Vicky, please," I say quietly. "Just let me handle this."

But she's already grabbing her coat. "You need someone in your corner, Jane. You can thank me later."

***

Alice's café is bright and cozy as always, but it doesn't have the same comforting effect on me as usual. It's like I'm floating somewhere outside my own body, observing everything from a distance rather than experiencing it myself. Nathan's already there, sitting at a table in the far corner, looking up with that easy smile that makes my heart flutter normally.

But the moment he sees Vicky at my side-the smile falters. *Oh no.*

"Jane," he says, rising halfway from his chair. "You brought a friend. Hi, I'm Nathan." He sticks his hand out to greet her.

Vicky doesn't accept his hand or give him a chance to say more. "So," she says, voice sharp and carrying across the room, "how long have you been stalking her?"

Nathan blinks, sinking back into his chair. "I-I'm sorry?"

"Don't play dumb. You know about her regular café, you leave little gifts at her home address, you somehow 'just happened' to come into the library to sign up for a card that time-how exactly did you find out so much about her so quickly, Nathan?"

His face goes pale. "I-walked her home when-" He looks at me, bewildered. "You suggested this place for our first date on Monday, remember?"

"I-yes, I did," I say, my voice barely a whisper.

But Vicky barrels on. "You're manipulating her, making her feel like you're this safe, caring guy when really you're sick. Obsessed. She's too trusting to see you for who you really are, but I'm not."

Nathan's expression is somewhere between hurt and disbelief. "Jane, is that what you think of me?"

I shake my head, but my throat is locked. Words won't come. I'm too frozen, too ashamed, too overwhelmed by the echo of every criticism I've ever faced.

The regular buzz of the café goes quiet. Alice looks up from behind the counter, frowning when she approaches. "I'm going to have to ask you to take this outside, Vicky," she says to Vicky in a hushed yet firm voice. "I hope you understand."

Vicky huffs, muttering something about "just trying to protect her," and how she's "said all she had to say," and grabs my wrist. Ugh, this is so embarrassing!

"Come on," she says. "We're leaving."

Nathan calls my name, softly, desperately, but I can't bring myself to look back. My heart feels like it's being torn in two-one half reaching for him, the other shrinking under the weight of everyone else's voices.

By the time we're out on the pavement, the sunlight feels too harsh, the air too cold. I let Vicky march me down the street, numb and silent, while behind us, the door to Alice's café swings shut with a quiet chime that sounds far too much like goodbye.

*** Nathan ***

For a few seconds after the door closes behind them, I can't move. The echo of her name still hangs in the air - the one I said, which she left unanswered.

Alice's café, usually filled with chatter and the hum of the coffee machine, feels too quiet now. Even the paintings on the wall seem to judge me. Until slowly but surely, the other patrons pick up their earlier conversations again, underlining just how alone I am.

I sink back into my chair, staring at the half-finished cup of coffee and uneaten brownie in front of me. Everything's gone cold. My appetite has waned. I no longer want either.

Alice appears beside me, resting her right hand gently on my shoulder. "You all right, love?"

I manage a faint, humorless laugh. "Define all right."

She gives me that look - the kind only people who've lived a little can pull off. Kind, but unflinching. "That was rough. Someone hasn't yet learned the difference between protecting someone and controlling them. Your girl Jane looked completely railroaded back there."

"She's not my girl," I say automatically. "I don't know what she is anymore."

Did a part of me expect this thing between us to blow up? Yes, eventually. Maybe a few weeks or months down the line. Not like this and not now. But somehow, I'm not surprised, just... numb.

Alice hums, resting her hip against the counter. "Maybe. All I know is she looked scared out of her mind."

I glance over at the empty chair across from me - the one I'd hoped for Jane to be sitting on by now. "Yeah," I say softly. "She was scared. I don't know of what, though. I haven't done any of those things her friend said."

Alice shakes her head, slowly. "Of course not. You would never. And anyway, I told you she works at the library. You didn't spy on her or anything like that."

"I realize how silly it sounds, but I thought she was

the one, you know?" I swallow hard, remembering her wide eyes the first time I kissed her - the way she'd melted into me one second and flinched the next, like she'd done something wrong just for wanting it. "She told me she loved me this morning. Just like that, out of the blue."

Alice sighs. "Sounds like you guys did move pretty quickly. I'm not judging, though. Sometimes lightning just strikes. I've seen it happen before. It was the same with Jack and me."

"Yeah," I murmur. "I guess sometimes things don't work out no matter how badly you want them to." I grow silent, trying to analyze every little moment we've shared over the past week. That first night at the Hart; our dinner date and her quiet confession after she'd invited me home…

You're the first.

Is that why she's scared? Is that why her friend is so protective of her? Because for whatever reason, she'd never-

It hits differently now. Maybe I should have been more careful. More patient with her. I definitely overstepped this morning when I kissed her on my doorstep. Though she seemed perfectly okay with it at the moment, I still broke my vow that I wouldn't pressure her.

Alice's expression softens when I shoot her a sad smile. "Sounds to me like you really care about her."

I nod briefly, eyes now fixed on the doorway. As if I could make her come back through sheer willpower. "I do care. Ah, I guess I'll get over it eventually."

Alice pats my shoulder again. "You're a good guy, Nathan. Jane's the one who's missing out."

I nod in silence. Not because I necessarily agree with her, but because it seems like a natural way to end the conversation.

By the time I leave the café, the surrounding bustle on the High Street lost its earlier charm and friendliness. I shove my hands into my jacket pockets and walk without much direction, just letting the motion steady me. By the time I reach home, my place doesn't feel like the peaceful sanctuary it used to be. It's empty. Deafening. Lonely. It doesn't help that her perfume still clings to the air around the couch. That may just be my imagination, though.

Three hours 'til my shift starts. Sooner the better. I could use the distraction.

CHAPTER FIFTEEN

*** Jane ***

Vicky's still talking. Or rather, ranting. Her words blur together into one long stream of noise that I only half-hear as she marches beside me, handbag clutched like a shield, or perhaps a weapon.

"...and you have to understand, Jane, these men know exactly what they're doing. They pick women who are sweet and trusting-"

"Stop!"

She freezes mid-sentence, clearly not expecting that tone from me. I stop too, right there on the pavement, my pulse thundering in my ears. I feel the adrenaline flooding through me, burning away the numbness that's weighed me down ever since we left the library.

"Just stop, Vicky!"

Her mouth opens, but I don't give her a chance to keep going. "I've listened to you long enough. You think you're protecting me, but you're not. You're doing exactly what my mother used to do-telling me that I don't know what's best for myself. Making me feel helpless!"

Vicky blinks. "Jane, that's not-"

"Yes, it is." My voice trembles, but I push through

it. It's time for the truth. The one I've never spoken aloud for half my life. "I never told you this, but when I was fifteen, a boy at school cornered me in the photography lab after class. He touched me, and I froze. I didn't even tell him to stop. When I told my mother what happened, she didn't comfort me. She called me a whore. Said I must have done something to make him think I wanted it. Said if I didn't want to be treated that way, I should stop acting so 'easy.'"

Vicky's face falls even further, but I can't stop now. Years of silence pour out. "Do you have any idea what that does to a person? Hearing that from your own mother? I cut her out of my life as soon as I turned eighteen, but couldn't shed her words entirely. I spent years making myself small and invisible because of it. Never dated. Never trusted anyone. I thought if I just stayed out of trouble, covered myself up in these big oversized sweaters and cardigans, I'd be safe."

I take a shaky breath, meeting her eyes. "Nathan was the first man I've ever even *wanted* to date. The first one I felt safe with. And you and your paranoia turned it into something ugly."

"Jane-"

"No, you listen to me." My voice cracks but grows stronger with every word. "I have liked him ever since that night when we went out to the White Hart together. After that night, I went there multiple times a week, just to see him. Never spoke a word to him; never even ordered a drink from him because I was so nervous. Until last week, when I stupidly tried to seduce him after one too many cocktails. I was terrified, Vicky! I wanted him with all my being, and I couldn't go through with it because I couldn't get my mother's voice out of my head all these years later. You know what he did when I freaked out? He backed off and told me he wanted to get to know me! And for the record, I told him about Coffee to the Rescue. I suggested it for our first date on Monday. We just ended up going to dinner instead."

Vicky looks stunned, her usual confidence slipping and her bottom lip trembling.

"And after that dinner, *I* invited him home. The first man I've ever had in my flat. Do you know what he did there? Or even last night at his place? Nothing. He didn't touch me, didn't push, didn't take advantage even though we were all alone, and he very well could have. He respected me. He's different. He's gentle and patient and-God, Vicky; he's not a creep or a predator. He's the first man I've ever had feelings for, and I'll be damned if I let you ruin that for me!"

Her eyes are wide and shiny with tears.

"I realize you must've had bad experiences with men," I add, softer now. "And I'm sorry for that. I really am. But not everyone's out to hurt us! Maybe you should talk to someone about your issues, instead of projecting them onto me."

My words hang heavily in the air between us. Vicky opens her mouth, closes it again, and finally exhales a shaky breath.

"You're right," she says, voice small. "You're absolutely right. I got carried away and stuck my nose where it doesn't belong. I let my own fears take over, and I'm sorry, Jane. I didn't know what you went through and I never meant to make you feel like your mother did. I just… I didn't want you to get hurt."

I nod, my throat tightening and eyes welling up too. "I know. And I'm sorry, too-for snapping. For some of the things I said just now. I have no idea what you've been through, either."

Vicky sniffles, then waves a hand. "Don't apologize. You were just telling it as it is. Usually that's my shtick. But you shouldn't dish it out if you can't take it, right?" She gives a wobbly smile. "It's all good. Hug?"

I laugh in relief as we wrap our arms around each other for a couple of seconds. "Thank you."

She nods and sniffles her tears away. "Now go. Go fix whatever I've just broken."

I don't need to be told twice. I turn and run, heels of my boots clattering against the pavement.

When I reach Coffee to the Rescue just minutes later, I'm out of breath and sweating despite the chill clinging to the damp autumn air. The chime above the door sounds a lot more urgent than normal as I burst in.

Alice looks up from behind the counter, her expression softening when she sees me.

"I'm so sorry about before," I gasp, scanning the room for him. "I didn't mean for any of that to happen."

She shrugs, unfazed. "Shit happens, love. Just don't let it happen twice."

I stare at the empty table in the corner, a plate with a brownie and espresso cup still sitting there, abandoned. "Where's Nathan?"

For a brief moment, I could swear she smiled. "He just left. That was quite the verbal thrashing Vicky gave him. Took him a moment to regain his composure. Poor guy."

My heart sinks. "Do you know where he went?"

"No idea, sorry." She hesitates, then adds, "Either work, or home?"

I nod, thank her, and hurry back outside.

The White Hart is my next stop, but when I rush in, Nathan isn't there, either. Just one grumpy punter at the bar and that female bartender with the attitude I usually ordered my drinks from.

My pulse hammers. That leaves one last option to try. The best out of the lot. If he opens the door and lets me explain, that is.

*** Nathan ***

When the doorbell rings, I almost don't move. I'm too busy stewing in my own thoughts when the sound of it ringing a second time forces me upright. I'm not expecting anyone, certainly not her. But what if it is?

Indeed, the vision of Jane standing outside my flat enchants me just like the last time.

Hair even messier than this morning, chest rising and falling with huffed breaths as though she's run the whole way here and up the stairs too. Her eyes meet mine, and for a second, neither of us speaks.

"Hi," she says softly. "I hope it's okay for me to turn up like this?"

"Jane. Yes, of course."

"I'm so sorry," she blurts out before I can say anything else. "For everything. For what Vicky said, for not stopping her, for just standing there like a bloody idiot while she went off at you-"

"It's okay," I mumble.

She shakes her head, frustrated. "No, it's not. It's *not* okay. You didn't deserve that. None of it. You've been nothing but kind to me, and I just... froze. I didn't know how to react. But you deserved to be backed up and defended. Not..."

I gesture behind me. "Won't you come in? You don't have to keep standing out here in the hall."

She exhales sharply, her shoulders deflating as she walks past me. I gesture at her to take a seat on the couch before joining her. She perches on the edge of the cushion, the same one she'd woken up on this morning, twisting her fingers together. "After we left, she wouldn't stop. She kept going on and on about how creepy it was that you knew where I worked, where I lived, my regular lunch spot. And I just… something in me snapped. I yelled at her to mind her own damn business. Right there in the street."

That draws a surprised chuckle out of me. "You did?"

"Yeah," she says, almost sheepishly. "I told her she's letting her own bad experiences with men run her life and ruin mine. I might have even told her she needed therapy. That was a bit… That was below the belt, I think. Just because some men have hurt her doesn't mean everyone-doesn't mean *you're* like that. And I told her that I'm sick of being treated like I can't make my own decisions. By her, by my mom, by-" She stops herself, drawing a shaky breath. "By everyone."

Her voice trembles on that last admission, and I feel something twist in my chest. No wonder she's so uncertain of herself if that's how life has been for her growing up.

"I want to tell you something else," she whispers. "Not to trauma dump on you, but… Just to explain, I guess?"

"Tell me anything," I say, folding my hands

together, just to give them something to do. She's so charged right now, it doesn't seem right to touch her or hold her. Though that's all I want, deep down.

"I want to tell you about why I panicked on Friday at the White Hart," she continues, sounding more determined again. "When I was in school, something happened to me. There was a boy … a couple of years older than me."

My mind races, because I already hate where this is going.

"It was late, most kids had gone home, but I was coming from the library and was walking past the photography lab when he cornered me and dragged me inside. There was nobody around… And he… Nothing happened, not really, he just felt me up a bit through my clothes, but I was so scared and couldn't make a sound. Not a scream, or even a single 'no.'"

My hand twitches and lands on my knee, right beside her. She reaches over and takes it, sighing as she waves her fingers through mine and squeezes them. I place my other hand on top, hoping that it helps.

"Afterwards, I ran straight home. I told my mom, but… She told me it was my own fault. That's what I get for dressing a certain way. I must have led him on. All that stuff. She'd never been particularly warm when I was growing up, very strict and unforgiving. But that… It shook me. Ever since that day, I tried my best to blend in. Stopped thinking about boys. Stopped… trying." She looks up at me, eyes bright with tears she tries to blink away. "So that's why I panicked. You didn't do anything wrong. It was never you. I just… froze, because I felt like I'd done something I wasn't supposed to, despite wanting it with all my being. And then I ran. Like always."

I swallow hard. "Jane-"

"No, please, let me finish." She exhales, gathering herself. "None of that excuses how I acted today. You didn't deserve to be humiliated like that. Please don't think that I believed a single thing she said. I never did, or I wouldn't be here."

I continue to cup her hands in mine. "If I did anything that made you uncomfortable, that night, or any other time, please-"

Her head snaps up and her eyes seek out mine. "You didn't. Not even for a second. You were perfect. You make me feel safe. You have from the beginning." Her voice softens then, tentative but sure. "And I meant what I said this morning. I love you. I know it was way too early, I know it sounds mad, but it's true. You're the first person I've ever felt this way about. Of course you're perfectly justified to change your mind in light of what happened today…"

The words hit me hard. They're everything I was afraid I'd never hear again.

"Never! Nothing anyone says could ever make me

change my mind about you." She turns to face me fully. Something warm floods my chest, fierce and protective all at once when our eyes linger on each other. "I'll do everything I can to make sure you always feel safe. With me. Even without me. I'll protect you as best I can. However long you'll have me."

Her lips tremble into a smile before she leans in and wraps her arms around me. The hug turns into something slower, deeper - the kind of kiss that feels like coming home. My heart continues to race and my skin glows with longing for her. Of course, I'll never act on it. I take my promises very seriously. None more so than my vow to keep her safe. From anyone, and especially from myself.

When she melts into me, I feel redeemed. Her arms cling to my shoulders, her lips can't seem to get enough of mine. It's the best. It's everything I hoped for, while also being still so pure.

By the time we pull apart, we're tangled on the couch, breathless, teary-eyed, and grinning like idiots. My hand finds her cheek, her fingers curl in my shirt, and for a second, I forget how breathing works. The look she gives me confirms: she trusts me. No matter what her friend seems to think. I've never felt more seen.

Time seems to stand still until I happen to glance up at the clock. "Shit," I mutter. "You were on lunch break. Don't you need to get back to work?"

Her eyes go wide. "Oh crap - yes! This is getting to be a habit."

We both burst out laughing, stumbling to our feet like a pair of teenagers caught sneaking around. She grabs her coat and I walk her to the door, unsteady, reluctant.

"You're working tonight?" she asks wistfully, standing up on her tiptoes to give me another long hug.

I nod, and shut my eyes while enjoying a whiff of her perfumed hair. "Sadly."

"That's not so bad. I can work with that." She smiles at me as she pulls away, resting her hand on my cheek one last time before turning around.

As she hurries down the stairs, I stand there watching her go. Wait, she can work with what, exactly? Puzzled, I head back inside, my chest filling with cautious trepidation.

CHAPTER SIXTEEN

*** Jane ***

I haven't been able to focus all afternoon and evening. Every time I shelve a book, I see his smile in my mind. Every time my phone pings, my heart skips.

It's not nerves this time. It's anticipation. The kind that curls low in your stomach and makes your hands a little shaky - not from fear, but from wanting.

I'm done letting the past dictate who I'm allowed to be. I'm done apologizing for feeling things that normal, well-adjusted people take for granted. The attraction between us isn't wrong or dirty. It's natural and righteous.

I realized it already a few hours ago, before Nathan rightly pointed out I had other places to be. I'm ready. He's been ready all along; the palpable tension in his body has been so obvious even when he's tried to be casual about it.

To know he wants me and has wanted me right from the start. And he still let me set the pace… that's priceless. Sure, he broke character a bit this morning when he kissed me. But I'd wanted him to all along, so that's okay.

He's nothing like Vicky said. He's a treasure.

Tonight, I'm going to show Nathan exactly what

he means to me. No ifs and buts. No stupid moral judgements and fears in my way. Tonight we're going to do what I wanted to but couldn't on Friday.

After work, I go home, shower, and stand in front of the mirror longer than I should - mascara, soft smoky eyeliner, the same pink lipstick I haven't worn since last Friday at the White Hart. No more oversized sweaters for me, I picked out a low cut top I would normally only wear as a base layer, and a set of pretty lace underwear to go underneath. The outfit isn't really provocative, but it's a lot sexier than my normal style.

I'm not "that kind of girl" anymore. I'm this kind of woman - one who loves, who feels, who chooses what's right for her, no matter what anyone else thinks or says. Tonight, I wholeheartedly choose Nathan. Not as Jane the boring librarian, but as a new me. Like a heroine in one of my favorite novels, I'm going all out for the man I love.

Old me was afraid of judgement, of doing the wrong thing at the wrong time with the wrong guy. But I no longer need to worry about that anymore. Everything is falling into place, because in his arms I'm safer than I've ever been.

By the time I walk into the White Hart, my heart is hammering so loudly, I barely hear the chatter around me. Nathan's behind the bar, sleeves rolled up, moving in that easy rhythm he always has. Except once he spots me, his facade slips. His eyes find mine, and wet glass in his hand slips and he barely manages to catch it again.

I bite back a smile. Adorable. Now that I've realized the truth, I can't unsee it anymore. Last time I was here, I was so wrapped up in my own insecurity. I never stopped to think that he felt exactly the same. It's crazy. Addictive. It also means that now I hold all the power.

Sliding onto a bar stool, I cross my legs, lean in and say, "Hey handsome, can I have the same thing as last time, please?"

He raises an eyebrow, pretending to play it cool, if not for the beads of sweat on his forehead and nervous tremble in his hand. Ah. Too easy.

"You mean the drink or the bartender?"

"Both," I say before I can stop myself. My cheeks burn, but the way his eyes linger on my lips distract from the heat.

He mixes the cocktail, though he's clearly flustered, even spilling a bit of it while pouring it out of the cocktail shaker. When he sets it down in front of me, I lift it to my mouth, never breaking eye contact. I wonder what else I can say to rattle his cage.

"You get off at midnight?" I ask casually.

There's a little shudder in his breath when he leans in slightly, voice dropping lower. "Yeah, how about you?"

My laughter erupts, too loudly. Alexis glances over from the other end of the bar, one eyebrow raised. The air between Nathan and me practically hums. He knows I'm not laughing at him. It's just this moment. I haven't had more than a sip, but I'm drunk with attraction.

It doesn't take a minute, some more customers come in. Alexis moves away, distracted. Nathan steals glances at me whenever he can. Luckily I took my time to get here. It's not that much of a wait. And even then, I could happily watch him mix drinks for the rest of my life. His movements, how his brow furrows in concentration. How his mask of stoic confidence seems to fall every time our eyes meet.

And yes, how absolutely smoking hot he looks in those very filled out jeans. Absolutely smackable. Squeezable. I can't believe this god of a man is all mine.

When the clock nears twelve, I slip away to the bathroom to check my lipstick - it's an excuse, really, to collect myself. Because this is happening. And I want to look like the sort of woman who knows exactly what she wants.

When I step back into the bar, the crowd and even the other staff has gone. The lights are lower, the music softer. Nathan's wiping down the counter, sleeves rolled up, looking good enough to eat.

He sees me and drops the cloth instantly.

We meet halfway, wordless, magnetic. My hands find the back of his neck and his breath catches just before our lips meet. The kiss is deep, hungry, but laced with tenderness - like we're making up for all the fear that once got in the way. And fanning the same flames that persisted all along.

When we finally pull apart, he rests his forehead against mine to catch a breath, and I whisper, "Thank you. For being everything I've ever dreamed of. I'm the luckiest girl in the world."

He looks at me like I've said something sacred. Like he's not sure he deserves it. Though he wants it. He wants everything I want. I see all my desire reflected back at me in the depths of his darkened eyes.

"Your place or mine?" I ask softly, immediately answering it myself. "Yours. My feet are killing me after wearing heels all day."

Before he can answer, Alexis appears from behind the bar with a knowing smirk. "Go on, lovebirds. I'll finish tidying, and lock up tonight. Just this once."

I can't help laughing. Nathan doesn't reply to her, or me, he just takes my hand, and we step out into the cool street together. We hurry through the fog like thieves in the night. There's no need to talk. No need to check in, because we already know we're on the same page.

Back at his flat, everything feels familiar and new all at once. The door barely clicks shut before we kiss again - slow at first, then deeper. My breaths can't seem to catch up, and my skin burns with need for his touch. We stumble toward the couch, the same one where I woke up wrapped in his arms this morning.

Now, I'm the one who takes the lead, fingers sliding up to undo the buttons of his shirt. His breath quickens, but his eyes search mine, steady and gentle.

"You sure?" he murmurs. "There's no rush."

I smile, tracing the edge of his jaw with my fingertip. "Nathan, I've waited my whole life to share this moment with you." Nodding downward. "Don't tell me you're not ready for this, too."

He groans under his breath. "Jane, I've been more than ready since Friday."

"You didn't…" I raise my eyebrows. "Blow off steam even once?"

His eyes seek out mine, burning into me with more intensity than even that first time. He shakes his head. "Didn't seem right."

"So this is all for me?" I whisper.

"Always."

I trail my fingers along the edge of his collar, teasing the fabric as I push it off his shoulders, revealing the plain black t-shirt underneath. Nathan shivers under my touch, the heat of him so close it makes my pulse hammer. I feel the strength in his arms as he wraps them around me to caress my back. I'm not afraid - not tonight.

With deliberate slowness, I tug at the hem at the bottom, revealing more of his thick, hairy torso as I go. I suck in a desperate breath when he fully comes into view. "God, you're gorgeous." He's everything I dreamed him to be.

My eyes catch the ink snaking up his bicep, the black swirls I spotted peeking out of his rolled up sleeve earlier turn out to be fragmented feathers and ash, the tail end of a beautiful fiery phoenix flying upwards to rise again. My fingers trace the lines religiously, memorizing each curve, each flick of ink. I lean down to kiss it. To kiss him. All the way up his arm, across his shoulder and the side of his neck before moving down towards his chest, where I bury my face in the short brown curls in the center.

He's so warm, inviting, and utterly perfect. And he smells amazing. I can't recall ever having seen a more beautiful man. Not on any book cover, starring in any movie or even in any dream of mine. To think that he's here with me is insane. I couldn't wish for anything more.

Nathan exhales sharply, leaning back just enough for me to straddle him, then end up on all fours on top of him. And still, he doesn't push. He doesn't rush me, despite the need I recognize in his eyes. I feel the familiar flutter of nerves, but it's different now - no panic, only anticipation and desire. This is our love, our moment, and I run it.

"Jane…" he murmurs, his voice low and raw with need. "How do you want me to touch you?"

I pause. "I… I'm not sure," I admit. Then I take a deep breath for courage. "Is it okay if I just touch you first?"

His grin is slow, fond, and entirely without reservation. "I'm yours to do with as you please."

I lean down, pressing my hands against the expanse of his chest, feeling the warmth of his skin beneath my fingers. Every curve, every dip, every inch of flesh is mine to explore. I see the faint tension of his Adam's apple, the way his hands twitch lightly on my thighs, holding but not guiding. This is a different power - a gift - and I revel in it.

The butterflies in my stomach have parted to reveal a steadiness I never knew I possessed.

I move entirely on instinct now. More kisses down his neck, caresses circling his nipples, enjoying the heat of his belly against my palm. Nathan arches toward me, groaning softly, and I feel a thrill that has nothing to do with lust alone. It's trust, it's love, it's finally being able to act without fear.

I realize I'm not panicking anymore. Not because I'm reckless, not because I've forgotten my past, but because I trust him, and he trusts me. He's giving himself to me completely. *I'm yours*, he said. I can't believe it.

Riding that wave of thrill and courage, I pull my top off, too, revealing myself to another for the first time ever.

Nathan's hands tighten on my hips. "Jane," he breathes, eyes searching mine, "you're beautiful."

I lean down to kiss him, softer this time, letting the tenderness melt into the heat. My hands wander until they cling to his sides, prompting him to wrap his arms around me. The fire of the phoenix etched into his arm mirrors the fire igniting inside me - alive, untamed, and reborn. Skin on skin, in his embrace I return home.

He shifts slightly beneath me, a shiver running through him when I feel the solid length of his erection press up into my inner thigh. I realize the full extent of the power I feel at this moment - the power to lead, to explore, to give and receive completely. "I love you," I whisper against his lips, "and I want this… all of it… with you."

Nathan groans, a deep, guttural sound, and pulls me closer, letting the words wrap around us like a promise. "I love you, too, Jane. More than I can say."

I smile against his mouth, leaning down to kiss him again, letting my hand travel down further this time, right onto his crotch, eliciting the most beautiful moan I've ever heard.

"God, I can't hold it," he gasps, causing me to

quickly withdraw my hand.

"Then we'd better take all this off now," I whisper.

CHAPTER SEVENTEEN

*** Nathan ***

She's a miracle. A dream. A fantasy come to life. And with a single touch, she has me gagging for release so bad, I feel desperate like a horny teenager all over again.

I vowed not to rush or pressure her, and I resisted it with all my might until I couldn't keep quiet anymore.

"God, I can't hold it," I blurt out. I'm so close, I see stars. Until she snatches her hand away.

I open my eyes to check if she's okay or I've messed it all up again.

"Then we'd better take all this off now," she murmurs instead.

And that almost gives me the last shove towards salvation. I try to hold on, though. The moment is just so perfect and I can't stand the idea of letting it slip away too soon.

Our first time, maybe. Or not. Our first bit of foreplay, at the very least. My first time surrendering myself to the woman I love. If this is all I get, if this is where it ends without me even finishing, it's still the most erotic and most beautiful experience of my life so far.

Crazy, considering I'm not exactly inexperienced. But still. She has me gasping for air just with kisses and caresses. And the view of her luxurious curves spilling out of pink lace, matching the lipstick she's transferred across my lips already.

I can't stand it. I don't know where to look or what to do, so I keep remembering her request. *Don't touch her. Let her touch you. Let her lead.*

It's fucking hard, bordering on impossible. But I do it. I resist. Who knew that would make this experience even hotter?

She lifts herself onto her knees above me, and gets to work on the button and fly of my jeans. It takes me a moment to catch up with her, fumbling with the same to get them off quicker so I can kick them off onto the floor.

"What about those?" She bites her lip and nods down at my boxers.

I open my mouth to ask if she's sure, but she silences me with an index finger to my lips.

"You'll stain them," she reminds me. Her tone is firm. Determined.

I nod in silence, and try to take them off too while she watches. I must look like a beached seal, flapping about awkwardly on my back. My erection springs free, and her eyes widen with a proud smile that spreads across her face, lighting me up from deep inside my chest.

I don't even care that I'm on full display and she's still wearing her bra and jeggings. My mistress is in control, and she looks pleased. That's all that matters.

"You really are close, aren't you?" she whispers.

I bite my lip and nod.

"What do you want?"

"Whatever you want to give to me," I say. ...*Mistress.* I add that last part in my thoughts, because I'm not sure she'd like it if I call her that. *Mistress Jane.* I've never had this particular kink before, but now, with her... I'm unsure I'd ever want to go back.

She shifts her weight onto her generous buttocks, inhaling deeply before gazing down at me again.

It's definitely different, having her in charge. It's also tender, loving, and mind-blowing. And it seems it's exactly what she needed to maintain the confidence she tried so hard to show last Friday and every time I've seen her since. My chest fills with warmth and I can't stop smiling. I want to tell her I'm proud of her, but that seems silly and patronizing. I'm in awe.

"What?" she demands.

"I'm proud to be yours," I say instead.

Her eyelids flutter as she exhales a soft moan. When she opens them again to look at me, she's even more determined. She gets up, resolutely casts off the rest of her clothes, and then retakes her place on top of me. "I want you. All of you."

"Yes."

"Nothing should get in our way," she continues.

"Never."

She settles her hips on top of mine, grabbing and squeezing my cock once, directing it up and into her. And then she bears down as if she knows exactly what she's doing. Maybe she does, on her own. Maybe with toys. Just maybe not with a man attached to it.

Maybe I should have worried about how to please her. About encouraging experimentation to figure it out. But she seems to know her body.

Hell yes. It's like coming home. If home was nirvana where hot slippery perfection awaits. She gasps when the head of my cock suddenly seems to slip past the first, very narrow hurdle. Her body grips me tightly, as if to say she's never letting go. And I can't breathe. Can't think. I want to move, to find release already, but I try my best to resist. My balls don't get the message, though, because they're trembling and contracting already. Her eyes snap open and lips part in surprise.

And just like that, she does exactly what I'd tried my best to stop. She starts moving. Her hips take a few tries to find a suitable rhythm. With her full chest pressed into mine, taut nipples grazing my skin while the soft curve of her belly brushes against me with every stroke. It's so sensual. So very beautiful. And so completely animalistic all at once. And I'd tried my damndest to hold on and last longer, but it's hopeless now. I'm gushing, spurting, releasing every last drop of cum into her. Before I get the chance to realize what happened, I brand her, marking her body with mine. She didn't even let me grab a condom. And yet…

I'm too overcome to protest.

It's just as I'd dreamed about so many times since I first saw her all those weeks ago. Back then it was a dirty secret, but now… It's righteous and loving. It was never about the sex. It was about being one with her. Gone is all my resolve. Hopeless are my efforts to remain stoic and strong. I'm reduced to nothing between her thighs. A shivering, sweaty mess of emotions. Tears pool in the corners of my eyes at the wild beauty of it all. When suddenly, she screams along with me. She collapses onto my chest just in time for me to catch. I wrap my arms around her as best as I can, cradling, caressing, and soothing her while she falls apart. I was already spent, but I still feel her body contracting around me. This is it. Our first time. Our first orgasm, shared.

"I love you," I whisper into her hair. "I love you so much."

I feel every word as I speak it. Tearing at my heart, convincing me that I can't ever say it enough. I'll try, though. I'll try for the rest of my life. I'll try to give her everything she needs.

She whimpers my name into the crook of my neck and digs her fingertips into my love handles.

"Shhh, darling. I love you," I repeat. Again and again, until her breathing slows and she settles comfortably into my embrace and her head resting on my chest. We're still entwined, a messy knot of limbs. Still connected, figuratively as well as literally.

The world feels smaller at this moment. Quieter. Like the night itself is sighing with relief.

I stare up at the ceiling for a long time, my hand tracing lazy circles on her back. I want to say something, but I don't trust my voice yet. There's a lump in my throat, and a strange ache in my chest - one that has nothing to do with desire and everything to do with what she's made me feel.

Wanted. Needed. Loved. Most of all, trusted.

From our very first flirtation, she'd conquered my heart. Although she was the one who expressed it first on Friday, *I* would have given her anything, too. My appreciation, my care, my love, even my soul. In turn, she gifted me her admiration, her warmth, her pleasure and her darkest secrets. It's only fair that I trust her with the same.

"Hey," I whisper finally. "You still awake?"

She hums so softly, it just about wrecks me.

I breathe her in - warm skin, faint shampoo, a hint of vanilla, and something purely her. It makes me dizzy. Because somehow, this woman I've stolen covert glances at for weeks, while assuming she was there for any other reason than me, is here now. Occupying my bed as well as my heart.

After everything she's told me about herself, I understand why things happened the way they did. And still, a tiny thread of insecurity won't let go. It's the final piece of the puzzle I have yet to share.

I tighten my arm around her and murmur, "I should probably tell you something, too."

She tilts her head up, nuzzling and nibbling on my ear. "What?"

"When you ran on Friday," I say slowly, "I thought it was me. That you weren't really into me. I still can't believe my luck even now. What you'd see in me."

Her expression softens when she pulls away to gaze down at me, but I keep talking before I lose the nerve. "You froze, and then you were gone, and I just… I figured I'd scared you off. Or that maybe you approached me as part of some kind of a dare or bet. Silly now, in hindsight, because dares usually require witnesses."

She blinks, stunned. "Nathan, you didn't *really* think that."

I let out a shaky laugh. "A part of me did. I'd admired you for weeks and couldn't understand why you'd ever approach a below average guy like me."

She pushes herself up, resting on her elbow, and

the sadness in her eyes melts me. "You're not just being humble, but you think that little of yourself? But you always look so confident, so in control of yourself."

Her voice is soft, but there's this fierce edge underneath it - protective, almost angry on my behalf.

I shrug, trying to play it off, but my chest feels tight. "You're… you. You walk into a room and the air changes. And I'm just a regular guy who serves drinks and reads philosophy books just to have something to say. Not exactly the kind of man most women dream about."

Her eyes soften. "You're wrong," she says quietly. "You're every bit the hero I like to read about in my favorite books and more."

That makes me chuckle. "I don't think there's ever been a romance hero with a beer gut and a growing collection of fantasy novels on his shelves."

She gives me a mock glare. "Stop it. Dad bod romance is my favorite genre!"

I wrinkle my nose. "That's… a thing?"

Her grin spreads, lazy and radiant. "It most certainly is. And you're way hotter than any cover model I've ever come across."

The words land deep. I feel my throat tightening again, but for a different reason now. I pull her closer, unable to stop myself, pressing a kiss to the crown of her head. Her hair's still damp against my lips, but I don't mind.

"God, Jane," I whisper. "You undo me."

She smiles against my chest, and the sound she makes - that little giggle, half-shy, half-happy - feels like the purest thing in the world.

"I hope you enjoyed your first time, even if I couldn't make it last very long," I murmur.

She tilts her head to look at me, eyes glowing in the dim light. "It was better than I ever imagined."

I swallow hard, brushing a strand of hair from her face. Because that's pretty much how I feel, too. "Yeah?"

She nods solemnly. "And you bet I spent a lot of sleepless nights imagining it. With you."

"Tease me like that at your peril," I growl, nuzzling her hair again. It smells so lovely. So *her.*

"Oh yeah? What are you going to do?" she teases.

I shrug. "Maybe try to give you another one of those orgasms." Catching myself, I quickly add, "Only if you're comfortable with that, obviously." *Whatever my mistress wants.*

I feel her smile into my chest while running circles around my nipple with her fingertip. "I'm willing to give it a try, in any case."

"Hey, didn't you say you had a tattoo, too? Where is it?" I wonder.

She raises her head and smiles at me again. "You won't see it from here, wait." She gets up and off of me before turning over until she's facing almost all the way away. I want to protest and pull her closer, but then I spot it on her shoulder blade.

"Ah, there it is!" I exclaim. "The key to my heart."

She chuckles. "Actually, the key to my freedom, but I guess it could be both from now on."

I caress the ornate old fashioned illustration with my finger. It's pretty and feminine, just like her.

"Freedom from?"

"My mom, mainly. I got it when I moved out the day I turned eighteen. Never spoke to her since." She shrugs it off, but it's obvious how monumental that moment was for her. After what she told me earlier, I can understand why she made that choice.

"Ah, tattoos are often like that, aren't they? To commemorate something pivotal," I say.

"Yours?"

"Got it after an old breakup that left me rethinking everything."

Jane turns again to wrap her arms around me and press her forehead against mine. "It suits you. I knew you were fire from the moment I first saw you."

Her turn to make *me* chuckle now. Ah, how easy it is to talk to her. How easy even to share those vulnerable parts of myself and trust she'll still see me, just as I see her. She's a whole lot more than the shy girl with the toxic mom, just as I'm more than the easygoing cheerful guy I try to play at work.

That's what love is, isn't it? To find someone you can show your true self to and know it will be accepted rather than judged.

For a few seconds, we just stare at each other. We marvel at the beauty we see in each other's eyes. And then… we find ourselves gravitating ever closer, our lips touching again, despite already being raw from before.

When I pull her against me, she seems to surrender completely. Skin on skin, her soft, exquisite curves pressed up against me. I continue to hold her, and will always cherish her. This is my promise to her as well as myself.

"You don't have to run anymore, okay?" I whisper. "I'll always keep you safe."

Her voice is sleepy now. "Wouldn't dream of it."

Just like last night, I tuck her into a throw and hold her as her breaths continue to deepen. It doesn't take long for the quiet hum of the city to fade into the background until there's only her.

I don't know what tomorrow looks like, but I know I'll wake up next to her. My Jane. My mystery woman, who I'll want to unravel every day for the rest of my life. And that's all I'll ever need.

EPILOGUE

*** Jane ***

Three months later.

I wake to the soft warmth of Nathan beside me, his arm thrown loosely across my waist and my leg draped across his thigh. And to my alarm, I quickly mute this unwelcome interruption so as not to wake him. It's still dark out, but the soft glow of the nightlight in the corner illuminates the outline of his tousled hair and the faint crease of sleep on his forehead. He stirs slightly, mumbling something unintelligible before opening one eye and smiling at me.

"Morning, beautiful," he rasps, voice husky with sleep. "Coffee?"

I stifle a yawn and nuzzle his chest. God, I'll never tire from the fact that he likes to sleep shirtless. "You've come to bed so late after your shift. Stay here while I make the coffee."

He groans, shifting closer. "You're too good to me, you know that?"

"Mm," I murmur, pressing a kiss to the corner of his mouth. "And you're too good to me."

I trail my fingers along his arm, then nudge him back down onto the pillows. "Stay."

"You're going to have to bribe me some more," he warns, half-smile teasing, half-serious.

I respond by leaning over him, brushing my lips across his ear and down the edge of his beard, planting soft pecks along his neck. He sighs, surrendering to the warmth of the bed. My fingers trace the line of his collarbone, over the solid plane of his chest, until I feel the steady rise and fall of his breath quicken beneath my touch.

His hands find my hips and pause there, waiting - always waiting, always letting me decide. I love that about him. That quiet patience that says: *I'll follow your lead.*

I shift to straddle him, my blonde hair falling around us like a curtain. The look he gives me-half wonder, half worship-makes something deep inside me unfurl. Once upon a time, I didn't think I'd ever do this, except in my imagination. I was too afraid, too imprisoned by old voices and judgements that hold no relevance anymore. But now… now it feels like second nature.

When I lean down, he meets me halfway, our mouths finding each other in a kiss that's slow and familiar and charged all at once. His lips part on a soft sound, and I swallow it, tasting sleep and warmth and him. The heat between us builds the way it always does - quietly, naturally, until the world outside ceases to exist.

He cups my face with both hands, fingertips brushing the base of my throat as if memorizing the rhythm of my heartbeat. I press against him in answer, the thin fabric of my nightshirt doing nothing to hide how much I want him. He feels it, too - I can tell by the small, involuntary sound he makes when I roll my hips ever so slightly.

"Jane..." It's barely a whisper, raw and full of reverence.

"What is it, handsome?" I murmur, brushing my thumb across his lips.

"Let me," he says, raising himself onto his elbows, lifting me with him.

This. This is how he gets exactly what he wants. With that same tenderness and kindness he showed me from the very beginning. I can't help but smile. This is another thing I couldn't have imagined at first. Another thing he taught me to trust: letting him take the lead, at least some of the time.

"I'm yours," I breathe.

"And I'm yours," he responds.

I'm not exactly petite, but as if by magic, he flips me onto my back and climbs on top of me. As much as I love riding him, it's a special kind of thrill when he spreads my legs wide and bears down on me. I wrap my arms around him again, reveling in the softness of his skin, all over his chest, his shoulders, his back, and his sides.

To think that he didn't realize how very attracted I was to him at first sight. That's lunacy. He's absolutely gorgeous both inside and out. And he's mine and mine alone.

Our reality narrows to skin and breath, to soft gasps and the faint creak of bedsprings as he moves on top of me - slow, tender, perfectly in sync with my every desire. When he gazes down into my eyes, there's no rush, no pretense. Just us, wrapped up in the kind of trust that took months to build and seconds to fall into each morning.

It never takes long, this time of day. Not because he isn't trying to last. He has built up such restraint and control that he could outlast me manifold. I'm the limiting factor. Me. We fit together so perfectly that every time he grinds down into me, I inch a little closer. Within minutes, I'm panting for release. And that's when I know how to take over. How to shift my hips just right, how to nip and lick at his nipples to drive him crazy.

He knows how to play me like a fiddle, edging me towards endless bliss. And I, him. I might have let him take the reins for now, but I'm not heading to salvation alone. I'm taking him with me all the way.

His eyes snap shut when I grab his ass, encouraging him to go harder. He's huffing already, which is always a good sign. Within moments, he'll be unable to stay quiet, making beautiful sounds that are somewhere midway between a moan and a grunt.

Those are my favorite. They mean we're exactly on the right track. And that's when he plays a little trick of his own, thumbing my nipple now. This never fails. It's building. It's coming.

"Oh my god, Nathan!" I cry out when the pleasure starts to pool.

He can't speak, only grit his teeth and carry on. And it's a beautiful sight. This big strong man, giving me his all. Harder, but not too hard. Faster, but not rushed. I wrap my legs around his thick waist, tilting upwards just right for him to hit that last spot. The one that lights me up inside.

And then… Oh god, and then…

"Holy shit!" He growls. He feels it. It's there.

"Nathan!" I scream.

He grinds to a halt, buried deep inside of me. And my body can't get enough. I cling to him with all my might, as if I could somehow absorb his body within my own. I'm trembling, shaking, gasping for air.

And he's my rock. Steady as usual, except for the shudder in his breath, and the pulsating of his cock. That always does the trick too, extending my orgasm just a little. Because there's nothing quite like the ultimate pleasure when it's shared.

When he finally collapses with his forehead on top of my shoulder, both of us trembling and breathless, he presses a kiss into my hair and murmurs, "I love waking up like this."

"Mm," I hum, still catching my breath. "I thought you were a night owl?"

He chuckles, a deep, satisfied sound that vibrates against my cheek. "I guess you've converted me."

We lie like that for a while - bodies tangled, hearts settling, and sweat drying. The quiet is full, not empty. That's new for me. Once upon a time, silence meant unease or judgement. Now it means peace.

This is what most mornings have turned into. Sometimes just the cuddles, sometimes a whole lot more.

It happens organically. Fingers and lips, exploring and loving whatever parts of the other that feel right. I confess to setting my alarm a little earlier nowadays, just to get the extra time with him.

After the very first time, I'd convinced myself that I was in charge. That I steered our encounters from start to finish. I could trust Nathan to never cross my boundaries, never pushing for anything that made me uncomfortable. But he's developed his own little techniques, his own ways to quietly coax me out of my old shell. It's as if we continue to discover new ways to appreciate one another, to show that we care.

"Gotta get up for work," I murmur between kisses.

Nathan hums, thumb brushing over my cheek. "Yeah? But it's only seven-thirty! Surely, we have time!"

I bite my lip and grin at him. "Busted, eh?"

"You've been waking up earlier lately," he speaks solemnly, but the little dimple on his cheek betrays his amusement. "Only to leave for work at exactly the same time as always. It's rather curious."

"Just to get more of this! Of you." I wrap my arms around his shoulders and enjoy the feeling of our bodies pressed up against each other. This closer contact gets my heart racing all over again. His fingertips dance lightly across my shoulders, down my spine, and land on my backside. He knows I can't resist that. I scoot closer and hook my leg around his thigh again.

"I'm certainly not complaining," he says. "And anyway, they say morning exercise is the healthiest of all."

"That's all this is to you?" I raise an eyebrow in feigned shock. "Exercise?"

"Ah, no, it's actually pure magic. The exercise element is just an added bonus." He grins at me, which I can only answer with a peck to his lips.

"So, what's on the schedule for Mistress Jane today?" he asks.

I laugh, rolling my eyes. He started calling me that soon after our first time together, when I insisted on taking full control. It's all in good fun. "Your Mistress Jane won't come out to play again until tonight once you get home. At work it's just regular old librarian Jane."

He chuckles, leaning his forehead against mine. "How on earth will I get through the entire day without you? Let's meet at Alice's for lunch so I don't get withdrawal symptoms."

I nuzzle his shoulder. "That would be lovely. I'm organizing a children's reading event today. The kids are excited, and I'm excited. It's going to be fun, but also… They're a handful, so I could really use a proper caffeine break."

Nathan's grin softens as he presses a kiss to my temple. "Glad to be of service. Twelve-thirty?"

"You know it."

We linger under the covers a little longer, talking, breathing, reveling in each other's presence. Sharing the quiet comfort of knowing we're in this together.

Eventually, I heave a reluctant sigh. "I should probably get going before I get late and the kids start wandering in before I get the chance to set it all up."

He groans dramatically, nuzzling me once more. "Fine, fine. But just so you know, you're making me miss you already."

I press a quick kiss to his lips. "You'll survive. And so will I."

Then, I slip out of bed, hurriedly have a shower, and get ready. By the time I gather my things to head off to the library, Nathan has drifted off asleep again.

Adorable. I could stare at him for hours. Instead, I snap a picture for me to admire later on.

***

When I reach my desk just minutes before nine, and put my bag on my desk, I notice something tucked neatly inside. Curious, I pull it out - a small ring box. *No way!* I open it, and inside is a white gold ring with an intricate Celtic pattern across the top. Etched on the inside of the band, in ornate cursive: *Be mine forever?*

A smile spreads across my face, warm and unstoppable. My fingers trace the delicate ring, and I can't help but think back to how this all began all those months ago - me, nervously lurking at the White Hart for weeks, silently watching him work. So convinced, I'd never have the courage to speak to him, nevermind much more than that. How certain I was that he'd never notice me. Funnily, he had all the same assumptions holding him back, too. And now… I brush my fingertip across the beautiful design adorning the band. It's so… him.

"That's beautiful. Early Christmas gift from Nathan?" Vicky leans over my shoulder to inspect the ring in my hand.

"Have a look at the inscription," I tell her.

Her expression shifts ever so slightly when she reads the words. "Holy shit, is this a proposal?" she asks.

I sit back in my chair and try to gather my thoughts. "Uhh…"

"'Be mine forever' sounds an awful lot like a proposal to me," Vicky doubles down.

I look up at her still smiling and unable to form a coherent response.

"Oh my god, Jane!" she squeals.

She drops it back into the palm of my hand, clapping as she does so.

"Well, what's your answer? It's a yes, right?" she asks.

Who are you and what have you done with Vicky? The same Vicky who told me Nathan was no good for me, and we were moving way too fast. Oh yeah, she's had a change of heart, along with what feels like a complete personality transplant, ever since she started dating Frank last month. It's been quite the shift, honestly. Good for her.

"I…"

"Tell you what. I'll look after the kids for Story Hour this morning, and you just sit here until you come up with a fitting response, okay?" Vicky pats me on the shoulder. "I'm so excited for you guys! Congratulations!"

Excited doesn't quite cover what I feel. I am, of course. I'm also moved, a little nervous, but mostly just… content. My answer isn't even up for debate. I was certain about him after our first date, and as I've gotten to know him better, and he's gotten to know me, I've only become more certain. Ugh, that's not even a thing, *more* certain. Like *more* perfect. But I can't think of any other way to describe it.

He's it for me. That's why we moved so fast. From strangers to living together just a month or so into our relationship, learning to love each other's annoying little habits, sharing our mornings before I go to my work and our nights after he comes back from his. Along with lazy lunches, weekend outings and two date nights a week on days he has the night off. It couldn't get more perfect than that. Except… with this ring on my finger.

From tentative glances and imagined conversations to this - a life that feels whole and fearless, full of love and trust. Now, this ring is a promise of forever: the next chapter in our love story, written one day, one moment at a time, but always together.

My answer to him is not just a 'yes,' it's a 'hell yes.' Rather than head to Alice's for lunch, I might just have to shift gears. Maybe I'll text him that I'll meet him at home instead.

Perhaps I'll have to let Mistress Jane out to play a little early today…

***

AUTHOR'S NOTE

Thanks so much for reading *Bartender Beefcake!*

Perhaps you've been following me for a while, perhaps you're new to my work. But now that you're here, I'd like to give you a little background on how this book came to be...

My writing career started all the way back in October 2012 when I took a very deep breath, closed my eyes, crossed my fingers and even my toes and clicked 'Publish' on my first short story. That steamy little piece called *Ladies' Day*, and the book it grew into eventually (Beautiful Stranger) are still relevant today because it features a curvy heroine and her more mature lover. It serves as my first foray into steamy body positive romance.

Since then, I've published a whole bunch of books, in various romance sub genres; as L. Moone I write contemporary, and as Lorelei Moone I write about shifters, vampires and other paranormals. Certain themes tend to repeat themselves throughout my catalogue.

Beauty lies in the eye of the beholder. The hang-ups we tend to have about ourselves and our bodies often aren't shared by the opposite sex. While it's a lot more popular to write about gorgeous curvy ladies and their athletic admirers than the other way around, I've always written both. I just never felt there was a big market for husky men in romance (my sales numbers supported this notion, unfortunately). 2020 changed that thanks to Jessa Kane and her sexy big boy titles, *Hefty* and *Husky*. My mind was blown, and I absolutely devoured them and couldn't get enough. I'm slowly seeing other authors enter this space, so perhaps the time has come? I hope so, because I could write about dad bod heroes forever...

Back to this book.

The beginning for *Bartender Beefcake* came to me about a year or two ago, but it wasn't until I finished *Roommates with Benefits* earlier this year, that I realized the sexy bartender in this story is none other than Nathan, who appeared as a side character in that book. After a bunch of grumpy/sunshine stories in a row, I ended up with a cheerful golden retriever hero who deserves all that is good in this world. And in his case, that's Jane, who recognizes his kind soul from afar and instinctively knows she can trust him with her heart as well as her soul. They're made for each other and know it right from the start in true Instalove fashion!

As such, the book is set in my Teddington story world, and we spend a lot of time at the White Hart, where Nathan tends bar, Alice's coffee shop, and a new location; the local library. Recurring characters from other books include Alice, Alexis, Megan and Dean. And I've got a new character, Vicky, who admittedly doesn't make the best first impression in this book, but let's just say she takes Jane's harsh words to heart and does some serious work on herself before we meet her again in *Coffee Shop Catfish,* which I'm going to launch in 2026.

If you've already worked your way through my backlist, do consider signing up for my newsletter (I'll give you a free book if you do!), and you'll be among the first to know when *Coffee Shop Catfish* releases. :-)

And that's enough from me. I hope you enjoyed the story as much as I did while writing it.

x, Lorelei

FIND ME AT:

- LMoone.com
- Lorelei Moone on Facebook
- AuthorLMoone on Instagram

I also write Paranormal Romance as Lorelei Moone. Check out LoreleiMoone.com for more information.

SPECIAL OFFER!

For a limited time, all new mailing list subscribers will receive a FREE book.

Claim your free copy here:

LMoone.com
Look for the newsletter sign-up form at the bottom of the page.

Printed in Dunstable, United Kingdom

78919343R00107